HOUSE OF WOLVES

A THREE LITTLE PIGS LOVE STORY

G.M. FAIRY

ISBNs: 979-8-9914470-5-8 (paperback),

979-8-9914470-6-5 (e-book)

CONTENT WARNING

House of Wolves may not be suitable for all readers. For a full list of content warnings, please visit gmfairyauthor.com

PLEASE NOTE

House of Wolves can be enjoyed as a continuation of The Wolfish Love Stories or as a stand-alone. For a better understanding of some of the characters' backstories, please read *The Crimson Wolf: A Red Riding Hood Love Story*

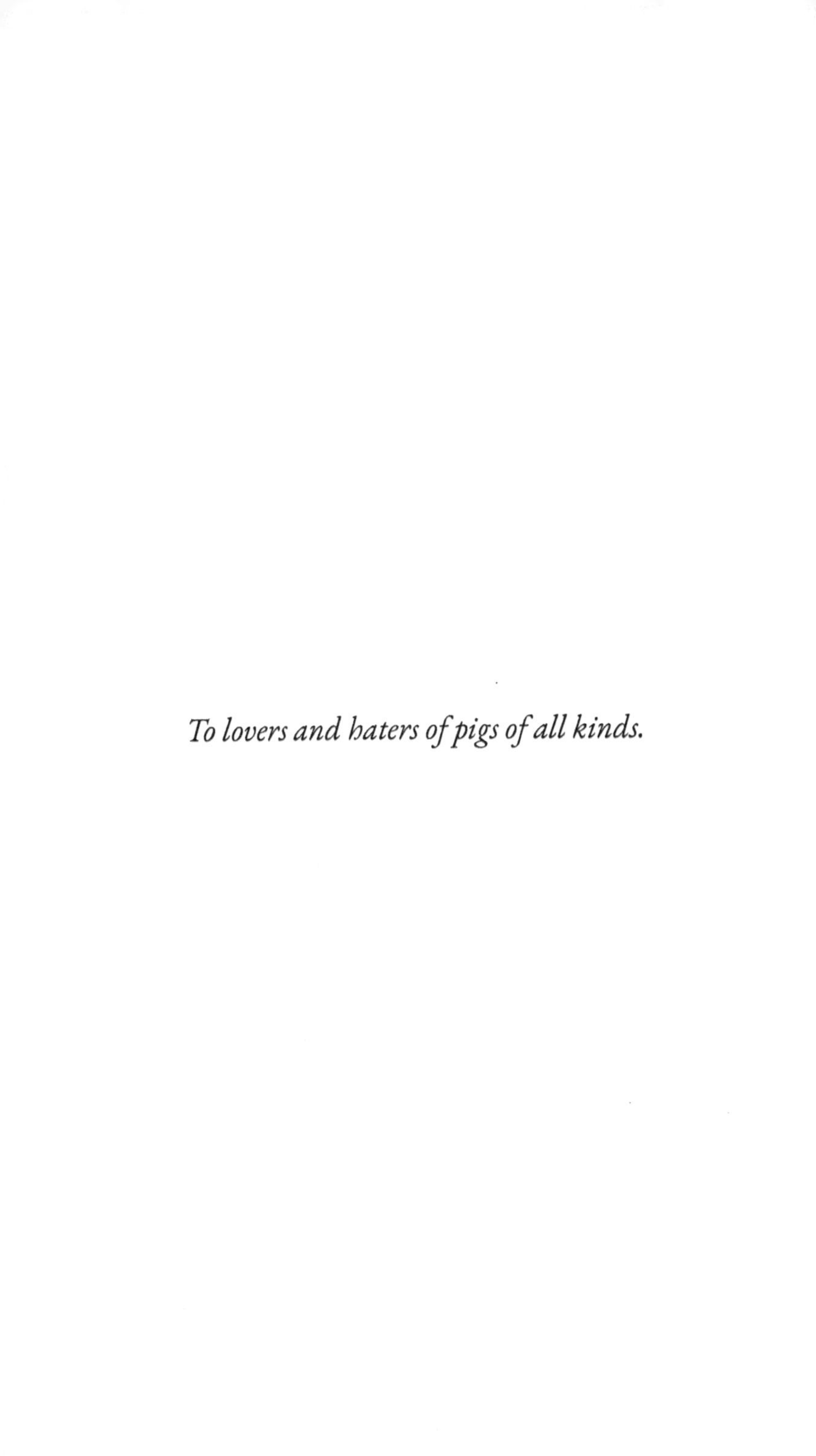

To lovers and haters of pigs of all kinds.

1

PIGS IN SHEEPS' CLOTHING

My bloodline is the stuff of legend—teeth and fury—but my inherited strength can't compare to the power behind the written word. It's not like I'm a stellar writer or anything. My training comes solely from growing up reading graphic novels and writing fanfics of my favorite characters. Still, as I sit in my cramped office, typing away at my keyboard, pure magic pours from my fingertips.

With just a few simple characters strung together by patterns, I can tear down an age-old evil group—one that discriminates, works to eradicate, and tortures my people. Okay, maybe it's not that simple, but it's more than I've been able to accomplish with my claws.

I skim over my latest completed article before sending it to my editor. Seeing the name *Gerald Howard*, a name I've written a dozen times, still sends a shiver down my spine. Just another public face for the Hunters, the group that has stalked my kind for centuries. The bulbous man is one of the wealthiest in town and the owner of Sentential Banks. He embezzled millions of dollars under the guise of his *Ending Hunger Charity*. This article isn't going to bring the Hunters to a halt, but it's something.

My time at the Dayton Daily as an Investigative Journalist consists of writing smear articles that work to break down the power the Hunters hold in their public lives. But this next piece will make the difference we've been waiting for. Werewolves will no longer need to hide in the shadows. I pull up my working document, thankful to be done with my assigned work and have some time to work on my real passion project.

"Carmen? What are you doing here so early?" I jump out of my skin, knocking my knees on the bottom of my desk. "Shit!" I yell, holding my hand over my heart. I turn my rolly office chair around, glaring at the voluptuous redhead in my doorway.

She laughs. "Didn't mean to scare you. I thought you would have heard me come in."

"No," I say in between a labored breath. "I was focused on my work."

She steps in. "Well, I can't say I hate that." She leans down to get a look at my screen. I cover my laptop with my arms. "Um, fuck off. It's not ready." Most people wouldn't talk to their boss this way, but Red isn't just my boss. She's my sister-in-law, married to my feral brother, and also, most importantly, my best friend.

She crosses her arms and raises her perfectly manicured eyebrow. "You don't usually mind me reading your work in its early stages." Shit. She's catching on to me. Red gives me creative freedom, but the article I'm currently writing is dangerous. As Lady Liaison, wife of the protector of the werewolf community, she'd have some harsh words to share if she knew how much I plan to expose in this article.

For centuries, werewolves have remained hidden. Not just because the Hunters have some demonic, obsessive need to end us, but also because regular humans don't necessarily love our furry behinds. I blame the media for our monstrous representation because, surprise, surprise—most of Hollywood is owned by Hunters. There must have been some smoking hot werewolves that turned down a white-fluffy-wig-wearing incel long, long ago, and the fucker decided to make a whole clan set on destroying our kind. No one knows exactly how the rivalry started, but the Hunters sure have a generational obsession with destroying us. Of course, there have been some bad eggs—werewolves born with a couple of loose screws or a shitty upbringing, but overall, we're just like everyone except with sharper teeth, furrier skin, and a waggy little tail. Most of the time, all these extra bits are hidden away. Thank God we can shift, or we would have been long extinct.

The fact is, the unknown scares people. We're different—rare and wield supernatural abilities. People don't like unchecked power. If only they knew how many evil people there were ruling everything under the guise of a civilized democracy. People would shit their pants. That's what journalism is for—to bring to light the dirty secrets the law tries to dust into dark corners. I'll forever be thankful to Red for moving to this shitty town and starting this local paper. If she didn't offer me a job, I'd still be waiting tables and fucking around until I found my calling.

This is why I feel so bad hiding something from her. I can't keep a secret from *anybody*. It's like I've been cursed never to lie; even when no one asks or cares, I spill all the itty-bitty details anyway. I'm a professional yapper. Literally. I get paid to yap but in written form.

"Fine! I'll show you!" I say as if she's been hounding me for hours, but in reality, she doesn't even cross her arms or give me a stern look. I sigh, moving out of the way so she can see my screen. She smiles and rolls her eyes, before shuffling to my laptop.

I pick at my chipped red fingernail polish as she reads. Thankfully, she's a fast reader, and my nerves don't eat away at my insides for long. "Carmen!"

"What?" I shrug, puffing my face.

"What is this?"

"It's an article I'm writing." Growing self-conscious, I move in front of her and pull my laptop against my chest.

She sighs, pinching the freckles on the bridge of her nose. "We've talked about this. Your brother…"

"Fuck my brother!" I yell.

"Wow, thanks, sis. I didn't know you cared so much about my sex life." Cameron steps into the doorway.

"What are you doing here?" I ask, crossing my arms over my chest and glaring at him. My whole life, people compared me to him. We knew he'd be the Human Liaison since childhood—the personified treaty between the Weres and Hunters. Werewolf identities remain hidden. All except the Human Liaison, who would show even from an early age that they were the most powerful. He couldn't be hurt, or the police would step in. Since coming into adulthood, he has worked as the middleman, speaking for his people to the select government officials who knew about us and protecting us from the Hunters who tried to learn more about other werewolf identities.

Of course, it was always known I was his sister. Even if it wasn't common knowledge and we didn't live in the same fucking house, it would be obvious. People thought we were twins once we started to level out in our ages—both dark hair, dark eyes, and tan skin. Even though I didn't receive the honor that comes with Human Liaison, I received all the consequences. My livelihood isn't protected, so I spent my life learning to fight harder than anyone else and never getting too comfortable. It didn't leave a lot of time to pursue other ventures. Although I dreamed of moving out of this god-forsaken town and starting fresh, I never had the means or opportunity to do so. I love Cameron. He's a good man and a good brother, even if he is a major pain in my ass, but God is it hard not to resent him. If only he didn't have to be born with so much power.

"He drove me," Red replies to my question about Cameron's mysterious appearance at our place of work, even though it's not that mysterious. He's always fucking here. Ever since they paired up and married two years ago, he won't leave *my* best friend alone. He has a *real* job as a park ranger, but damn, it sure seems like our parks don't need a lot of rangering because he's up her ass like a butt plug. Okay, wait, ew. I don't want to think about my brother and butt plugs. Thankfully, Red carries on, bringing my attention back to our conversation. "I'm working from home today. The doctor said I need to start taking it easy. I'm just here to get some things."

My eyes lower to her obviously large belly encasing my niece. Right, I always forget she's pregnant. It's not like she isn't showing. She is eight months pregnant and looks like she's about to pop, but Red never stops. She's always working, always scheming about making the world a better place for her baby. Her baby werewolf.

I pop to my feet. "Shit. Please sit," I say, motioning to my chair.

She holds up her hand. "No, it's okay. I'll be sitting all day. It's good to get *some* time on my feet." She shakes her head, rubbing her temples. "But Carmen, focus. We've talked about this. We can't just use this paper to expose the Hunters explicitly. We'll lose our credibility without hard evidence to back up our claims, and the minor offenses of the Hunters will be pushed under the rug again. We have to wait for when the time is right."

Cameron tsks, leaning against the wall, pinning me in place with a stare and a smirk. "You should write her up, boss lady."

I ignore him, rolling my eyes. "Red, it's been two years, and besides, we have evidence. We have the recording of Jack admitting to the murders in the clearing."

Red didn't just come to Dayton, Washington two years ago for the scenery. She was an investigative journalist for the New York Times, sent back to her hometown to investigate mysterious murders reported in our woods. The victims were werewolves, murdered by Hunters but staged to look like they were regular people killed by werewolves or, more publicly, killed by animals. The problem with a whole group of people having secret identities is that no one knew they were Were except for our own. The police pushed it under the rug and sided with the Hunters, but then Red showed up and, with some help from my idiot brother, got one of the main culprits in the murders to admit his involvement before Cameron ripped his throat out. The confession was recorded and handed over to the police.

"Sergeant Brick doesn't want us to use that recording yet. He said it's not time."

My face heats. "Fuck that pig!" I yell. Okay, maybe I'm being a little harsh. I don't necessarily hate police or anything. Even if it seemed they had taken the side of Hunters over Weres throughout our history. In fact, I've hooked up with a few of the officers and even have a friend who works as the office administrator at the station that gives me inside information. Believe me, I'll be the last person to hate an entire group of people blindly, but I mean it when I call Brick a pig.

Sergeant Brick is one of the newer editions to the police force. He has connections with the National Department of Supernatural and seems to be sent to Dayton to fix our unequal power dynamic. The Werewolf Council has even accepted him into our pack, inviting him to meetings and sharing *way* more information than anything we've ever shared before. Cameron and Red think he's part Were or something, but I can't smell it on him. There's definitely a strange aura about him. The air thickens when he's around, as if magic coats his skin. But wouldn't he admit to us that he's a werewolf if that were the case? I don't trust him as far as I can throw him, which is saying a lot because he's *well* over six feet tall.

"Carmen, he's on our side," Cameron butts in.

"We don't know that. It's been three years, and no Hunters have been arrested for those murders."

"There also haven't been any more murders of werewolves. It could be because of our articles or because Brick keeps things in check behind the scenes," Red says.

"Or they could be planning something more sinister."

Red sighs, and I notice the dark circles under her eyes for the first time. "I sure hope not." Her shoulders seem to sag under the weight of the world. Cameron rushes to her side, rubbing her back. I'm a dick. I shouldn't be arguing with her in this condition. Instead, I should agree to her rules and ask to rub her feet, but I'm just so tired of letting powerful people get away with horrible things.

Cameron speaks up, his eyes stern. "Carmen, don't waste your time on this article. We have a council meeting tomorrow. At least bring it up there before you do anything stupid."

I nod, not feeling my spunky self anymore.

Red smiles at Cameron and turns back to me. "I love how passionate you are about this. I want to stop the Hunters as much as you, if not more." She rubs her belly. "But we must work as a group and wait until everyone's on board with our next move. In the meantime, we keep the fire under their ass and enjoy the peace."

I nod. "Okay."

She smiles. "Alright, well, don't work too late today. That's an order. I need your help deciding on the nursery's wall hangings tonight."

I nod. "Okay, I promise. I'll be at your place by six."

"Good." She turns to leave. Cameron gives me one last scowl before following after her.

I slump back into my chair, staring at the blinking cursor before me. Am I really just going to put this article away and *listen* to directions? That's never been me. It's the most not me thing possible. I sigh, leaning forward and twisting my nose rings as I read through the last words I wrote. I guess I can wait to annoy everyone until after the baby is here and settled. It's the least I can do.

An email notification pops up at the top of my screen. It's from Lucy, my friend at the police station. Perfect. Just what I need. A distraction until I can get back to working on the real work. The email is from a string of random letters and numbers—a burner email. She probably would be fired if the station found out she was sending inside information to the press before it went public. Lucy and I used to work together at the diner. We've always been willing to break the rules for each other. Thank God because the only other option is hooking up with one of the two cops on my roster. They're a decent enough fuck, but a pain to be around without a stiff drink. I'd much rather be stuck in a room with them over Sergeant Brick, but that's not saying much. Regardless, I would prefer to get my info from Lucy.

The subject line reads: *NEW MURDER.*

My heart stops. I love getting dirt on Hunters—robberies, embezzlement, ripping people off, but murder is never a good thing. A murder most likely means it's someone I know. I click the email, terror swimming through my veins as I take in the image embedded in the message. It's a murder, alright. A young girl, barely into adulthood. Blood covers her head, and she lies on the carpet, her eyes lifeless.

I know this girl. Of course, she's not just a girl. She's a Were, just growing into her powers. The Hunters shouldn't have known her identity, but now we're more vulnerable. We let the police in because we thought hiding in the shadows had been too dangerous. Obviously, being out and in the open has its consequences, and a feeling deep in my gut tells me the violence doesn't stop here.

2

PIG TRAP

Nothing beats the feeling of the late-summer breeze slipping through my fur. The full moon shines overhead, lighting my path as I race through the dark and dense forest. Instead of focusing on the emergency meeting with the Werewolf Council, I try my best to stay in this moment—to focus on my breathing, my paws pushing me forward. Of course, I know what the meeting is about. I'm the one who called Grimm and told him the details of Stacy's murder.

The hidden council building comes into view. From the outside, it looks like an abandoned church—an old wooden building with vines crawling up all sides. The windows are boarded up, and you must travel several miles through the woods to find this place. We never share its location. The only way we can all find the building is that it's marked with our scent. Yes, we all piss on the side of the building. It's gross and undignified, but we are intelligent mythical dogs. We're going to be a little weird. I draw the line at butt sniffing, although the other males don't always share my sentiment.

I'm alone as I approach the door. My senses heighten, and I take in the environment around me. I twitch my ears, sniff, and stare into the darkened brush, vigilant that nothing gets past me. Satisfied that I'm alone, I enter through the rickety door, stepping into the small entryway, a rack of heavy cloaks to my side and a frosted glass separating me from the main room.

The glass is thin, and the chattering of familiar voices chirps around me—my fellow pack, all in their human forms, on the other side of the door. I shake the damp air from my fur and shift. It happens almost instantly, in the blink of an eye. As a child, up to my early adolescence, it was more difficult for me to switch between forms, but it's natural to me now, thanks to practice and growing into my powers. It's not as easy for everyone. Some only shift during a full moon. Some need training to control their transformations. Our family line is powerful. Cameron is the most powerful in the pack, a sentiment he *loves* reminding me of, but I'm close behind him.

I'm naked—an annoyance that comes with shifting. Unfortunately, our clothes don't magically change with us. I do look fucking fantastic naked, but it would be rude to enter a room full of people tits first. How could anyone concentrate? I remove a black robe from a hanger and slip the heavy fabric over my shoulders. To an outsider, it might seem weird that we're all wearing matching robes like some weird, comfy cult. But we're werewolves, the stuff of storybooks. This is the least odd thing about us. I bet some packs meet in groups naked, so considering that, we're pretty normal.

I step into the meeting room, the lighting low, and everyone sitting in old, wooden pews facing a stage at the front. "Carmen, good you're here," Grimm says from the front of the room. "I just filled in the pack

on Stacy's murder. Come tell us what else you know."
The silver-haired man motions for me and steps to the
side. He's the leader of our pack—the voice of reason,
level-headed and trustworthy.

I gulp before walking forward. I'm shit at public
speaking. I'm barely comfortable talking to people
outside my close group. Writing my thoughts for the
public is one thing. I can ponder my words before
spewing them to the masses. My mouth and brain
don't always connect as quickly as I'd like. I love to
talk, but not in such a serious setting.

I take my place before the small crowd—the people
I've known my whole life. Well, except for one guy at
the front. Never seen him before. I eye the blonde,
attractive newcomer staring at me. I have half a mind
to ask him who he is before I go on, but that would be
in poor taste considering the news I'm about to share.

"Well, I'm not sure what Grimm already told you,
but I got the email today from my inside connection
with Stacy's crime scene pictures. Her fingertips were
cut off." The audience gasps.

The email from Lucy contained more than just one
image—there were several photos of her living room,
the blood splatters, and close-ups of different wounds.

The Hunters usually leave a message. It's always different, but they like to make their handiwork known. To a regular person, missing fingertips would look like the signature of a demented serial killer, but to me, someone who's studied the Hunters' killing. I know what it means. They like to take off a part of us that housed our power. In Stacy's case, it was her claws. Now that she's dead and in her human form, no one would see the missing claws. All they see is missing fingertips. This was obviously a Hunter killing. The time of peace is over. Why couldn't they fucking wait for Red to have their baby? What major dicks.

The murmuring grows louder. I scan the chattering crowd as my brain finds the right words to continue. I catch Cameron sitting alone at the back. My heart stops, wondering where Red is. He nods at me. It could mean anything, but we have a weird sibling connection sometimes. He's reassuring me that Red is okay and at home resting. Of course, she's at home. If something was wrong, he sure as shit wouldn't be here. This would all be too much for her in her condition.

The audience's panic heightens, and I still haven't said anything to calm anyone down. I don't know what to say. I'm freaking out too. I connect my eyes with Grimm, widening them in a plea to save me. He should know by now that I'm not the type of person who delivers bad news. I don't have any soothing words—only the facts.

He sighs and stands, holding his hands up in a calming motion. "Everyone quiet down. We have gathered so we can all be informed and stay vigilant. There's more to share." He stands next to me. There's more to share? I sure as shit don't have more, and I'm the one with the inside information. Maybe Sergeant Brick is finally being useful. I doubt it, but I'm eager to find out. I stare at Grimm's profile, waiting for him to go on. Finally, he turns to me, eyeing me to take a seat.

Thank God. I shuffle to the spot he got up from, right next to the strange blonde. The guy gives me a polite smirk as I sit, closing his legs to give me more room. I nod friendly, but when he turns back to Grimm at the front, I lean in for a whiff. It would be a weird thing to do in any other setting, but this is a werewolf council meeting, after all. Werewolves sniff each other.

Sure enough, I sense the Were on him right away. That's a good sign, but I can't help wondering why he's here. We never get newcomers, and our numbers are constantly dwindling. His presence unnerves me.

Grimm's voice grabs my attention. "We've been keeping this information from you all until we had more concrete facts, but young Were women have gone missing."

What? How did I not know about this? It's my job to know the facts and spread the truth that can help keep our people safe.

He goes on, speaking over the rising murmurs of the crowd. "Lara, Summer, and Victoria have gone missing separately over the last two months. We weren't sure if they were just leaving town without telling anyone or if their disappearances had anything to do with the Hunters."

Of course, their disappearances have to do with the Hunters. Everything has to do with the Hunters. All three women are under the age of twenty-one. This can't be a coincidence.

Grimm carries on, "You may notice we don't have a certain Dayton Police Force member here today."

Oh, is Brick not here? Now that I notice, the air does lack its usually pig-filled scent.

"This is intentional," Grimm informs. "We've grown suspicious of the police's intention in our alliance. It's no secret that the Hunters' money and power have influenced the police before. We thought with our new connection with Sergeant Brick and his involvement with the National Department of Supernatural, we finally had an equal playing field, but now we have evidence to believe someone on the force is compromised."

"What evidence?" I pop up from my seat, unable to stop my bubbling questions.

My answer doesn't come from Grimm, though. The man next to me clears his throat. "I've been to the victims' properties. Everyone has had a common thread—hoof prints leading away from the house," he says with a slight Norwegian accent.

I stare at the man who just spoke, distracted by his clear green eyes, the slope of his nose, the uncanny perfection of his skin, and most of all, why the fuck he knows this.

"Hoof prints? So what?" I rebut.

"The police force has horses," he replies.

I scrunch my brow. "So? They could have been on a horse to investigate after the missing person's report."

"The police never came after the families called. When reported, they said the women probably just ran away, and there was no reason for alarm. The houses have been under surveillance since the women have gone missing, and no police have arrived."

I get what he's saying, but it still doesn't make sense. "Okay? Do you think the police stole the women on their own police horses? Wouldn't that be completely obvious?"

Grimm speaks up from the front. "All four women lived in secluded cabins in the woods. Horses would be the easiest way to transport them." He addresses the crowd now, and it jolts me back to reality. For a moment, I forgot I wasn't having a conversation alone with the two men. "Of course, many people in this town have horses, but the fact that the police are so adamant about the women running away and refusing to investigate, and now with the murder of Stacy and no public response on the incident, as if they are attempting to sweep it under the rug, signs are pointing to a police cover-up."

"What did Brick say?" Cameron asks from the back of the room.

The man next to me stands and turns to Cameron. "We haven't reached out to him, and he hasn't reached out to us, making us even more suspicious. The Hunters knew these women's identities. There are only a few ways that could be possible. Brick being the number one suspect."

"Okay, should I know who this guy is?" I ask, still on my feet and fed up that this random dude knows more than me or my brother—the fucking Human Liaison.

The blonde eyes me with a smirk, clearly amused by my annoyance.

Grimm speaks from the front. "I apologize. With everything going on, Kilo's introduction wasn't on my mind."

The man next to me addresses the crowd. "Hello, everyone. My name is Kilo Johansen. I arrived in your town a week ago. Mr. Grimm asked my pack for help dealing with your local Hunters. We had a similar situation years ago, and the story was highlighted in the National Department of Supernatural back interface. He wanted to see if I could help defuse what he feared was happening here."

Cool. Grimm thinks we're incapable of dealing with the Hunters on our own, so he begs some Europeans for help. I really don't care. I just want to know what the fuck is going on. I sigh. "Which is?"

"We think the Hunters are taking young werewolf women to impregnate and make powerful Hunters. This is what the Hunters attempted in my hometown." The crowd murmurs into panicked whispers.

I cross my arms over my chest. "Well, duh."

"Duh?" Kilo eyes me with a strange sparkle.

I sigh. Kilo's theory about impregnation isn't entirely new. "Two years ago, the lead Hunter captured one of our own. He admitted as much to her before *our* Human Liaison ripped his throat out."

Kilo nods at my words. "Yes, Grimm informed me of the incident. But he also said you have had two years of peace. It's suspicious that they're choosing to act now."

Cameron walks to the front. "Regardless of the timing. It's happening, and people are getting killed. We can only hope that the other three are alive and can be rescued." He stands beside Kilo, grabbing his shoulder in some macho man's embrace. I roll my eyes. "Thank you for coming, Kilo. We could use all the help we can get, especially from a Human Liaison who has experience ending a powerful hunter clan."

I sigh. "Okay, cool. So now you're here and know everything about stopping Hunters. What do you do about it?"

Kilo studies me, the curious smile not leaving his face. He steps closer, sending my annoyance off kilter. He smells of pine, and even though he's only a fraction closer, his beauty alarms me even more. "First, we need inside information," he says to me as if the other werewolves in the room don't exist. "Grimm tells me you have some inside connections at the police station."

"Yeah, I have my friend Lucy, but she just sends me reports that get passed over her desk. I doubt they'd privy her to their kidnapping plan."

He shakes his head. "No, I'm not talking about that connection. I hear you have past relationships with some of the cops at the station. This couldn't just be Brick who knows everything. Many cops would need to be involved."

My cheeks heat, and I whip my attention to Grimm. I don't care that he's my leader. Why the fuck is he spreading rumors to new people about who I fucked? And most importantly, how does he know?

Again, I remember that we're not alone. Thirty men, women, and young adults surround us. My dentist, the grocer, and people I've known my whole life bore holes with their eyes into the side of my face as we stand at the front and discuss my past hook-ups.

I furrow my brow, shifting my gaze from one male to another. "Gentlemen, this hardly seems like a time to discuss my dating history."

Grimm's eyes widen as if suddenly realizing the contents of the conversation. "Right. I apologize." He turns back to the crowd. "Everyone, we will end tonight's meeting so a few of us can work out the details of our next plan. What matters is that we watch out for our young women, stay in groups, and report anything suspicious. Do not panic. Do not fear. We are working on our continued safety and bringing our own home safe."

It takes a few minutes for the crowd to disperse, chatting with others anxiously before heading to the door and cautiously slipping out. Cameron, Grimm, Kilo, and I stand at the front of the room. We don't address each other until everyone has left. The last

Were slips through the entrance and kicks the door closed behind them. I turn to the men, arms over my chest and fire behind my eyes. "So now that my dating history is out in the open, please let me know who you'd like me to sleep with so we can get more information."

Cameron groans. "Carmen, calm down. It's no secret that you've fucked around with Officer Straw and Wood."

"It's not a secret, but this guy has been here what, five minutes, and he already knows who I've slept with before I even know his name."

Kilo bursts into laughter next to me, surprising my rage and diverting my attention from my annoying brother to the handsome newbie. He grabs Grimm's shoulder. "I like her," he says, pointing to me. I don't know if I should be annoyed or flattered that he enjoys my candor. Maybe if he wasn't so hot, it would piss me off more, but his laugh does break some of the tension.

Grimm shimmies out of Kilo's grasp. "Carmen, I did not disclose those details to Kilo. I didn't even know the finer workings of your relationship with the officers. All I said was that you had a friendship with the two."

"Oh." My face heats. *Fuck*. "Well, I guess we cleared the air. And yeah, if the two know anything, I could find out." I haven't met up with either of the men in a while, and I never feel too great about myself after seeing them, but if it's in the name of saving young women, I'll blow just about anyone.

Kilo puts a hand on my shoulder. I stiffen. "I'd offer to help, but it might be suspicious. I don't want you to do anything you're uncomfortable with."

My cheeks heat, and I brush a strand of hair behind my ear. "It's fine. I'd offer to do it anyway if it wasn't already suggested. The two are idiots. It won't take much for me to get something out of them."

Grimm claps his hands together. "Great, we'll start there. Let's meet back up after you've made contact. We'll meet at the cave, say, in two days?"

We own a hidden building within a cave nearby. The Hunters know this location. We use it to house prisoners, conduct small meetings, and for training. Only the most powerful werewolves visit its location as they can handle a Hunter attack. This council building is for everyone.

"Yep," I reply with a tight-lipped grin.

Grimm nods and shakes all three of our hands before exiting. I step closer to Cameron, whispering, "Does Red know about this?"

"Of course. I don't keep anything from her."

"Maybe spare her some details. I don't want this upsetting her in her condition."

Cameron gives an aggravated chuckle. "She's pregnant, not dying."

"I know, but the doctor said she needed to take it easy."

He steps away from me, his aggravation turning to anger. "Let me worry about my wife, and you worry about your cops."

I grab his arm. "Okay, calm down." But he pulls away from me and storms out of the building. I watch him leave, shaking my head.

"I'd assume you two were jaded lovers if you didn't look so much alike."

I give a disgusted look to Kilo, who I just remembered was still in the room. Why wouldn't he leave with Grimm instead of lingering around to listen to our conversation? What a weirdo. Maybe the culture is different in Europe, though. "Yeah, he's my brother and has a very pregnant wife at home."

"Ah." Kilo nods. "That explains it." It does. Male Weres tend to become completely irrational during their mate's gestation period. Cameron can naturally be a dick, and with Red being so close to her due date, he's almost intolerable.

"Yep." I nod before walking away. Sure, the guy is hot, and it's not like there are many men to choose from in this town—hence why I've hooked up with two cops—but I don't know this guy, and I already have a lot on my mind. I don't have the time to flirt.

He grabs my hand, and I turn back to face him. "I just wanted to apologize again. I didn't know the situation and didn't mean to embarrass or imply anything."

I wrap my arms over my chest—subtly hoping my boobs push out a bit from my robe. My plan isn't to seduce him, but I never miss a chance to be the object of desire of a male I'm attracted to. "Again?" I ask.

"Huh?" He steps closer, his eyes soaking me in.

"You said you want to apologize again. I don't remember you apologizing the first time."

His grin grows. "Ah, you're right. You don't miss a thing, do you?"

"It's kind of my job. I'm a reporter."

"Right. Well, I apologize for the first time."

"Thank you." I nod, turning to the exit.

He grabs my hand, his grip strong and his hands rough. "Now, you must let me apologize for a second time."

I smirk, becoming less annoyed and more amused. I size him up. Even though I can't see much from the robes, I can tell from the veins vining up his neck, the grip of his hand, the cut of his jaw, and his height that he probably has a good body. Yeah, he could be fun. "I'm all ears."

"Let me do it properly. Let me take you to dinner."

I rub my lip, making more of a show of studying him. "I don't know. I'm going to be awfully busy with my little pig trap, and you are here to train us to defeat Hunters since we are so pitiful at it."

He holds a finger up. "That's not why I'm here."

"Sure."

He doesn't let go. "But we both need to eat, and I'm sure there's plenty we can teach each other in our areas of expertise."

This could go on all day. I would like to sit down with him and discover why Grimm thought he was so valuable to ship across the world to help us. Of course, more help is always great, but why was he even willing? What's in it for him? Besides all that. He's fuckable, and after messing around with cop dumb and dumber, I'm going to want a fresh lay to feel better about myself. "Sure. We'll have dinner."

"Great."

I jump in before he can say more. "But I can't tell you when. I will be very busy being wined and dined by other men, so we'll just have to make plans after I meet with them."

"Sounds like a plan."

"A plan for a plan, but yes."

"I'll take it."

I hold his smile momentarily, and he finally lets go of my hand. Damn, Europeans are pushy. I wink before turning on my heels and exiting from where I came from. Half of me hopes he'll follow close behind so we can get a peek at each other before shifting into our wolf forms. But to my dismay, he's a gentleman, staying back and waiting until I've exited the entryway. What a fucking disappointment.

3

PIG MEAT

I have self-respect. I swear. But as I order a large chocolate milkshake and fries from the drive-through window over the lap of Officer Straw—Jeremy Straw—I question if my feminist ideals about equality have brought me too close to the sun. When he suggested this fast-food car date, I should have requested more, but I can't be too picky. I am only doing this to get information from him.

"I'm so glad you called," Jeremy says before shoving a handful of fries in his mouth, unaware of the chocolate smeared near the corner of his lip.

I take a sip of my milkshake, studying him in his navy blue uniform. His tight shaved head, his muscular form, the blocky set of his jaw—he's attractive, no doubt, but his looks only carry him so far. I wish we had met up at a bar or a restaurant where I could order a drink. I like him a hell of a lot better with alcohol swimming through my veins.

I smile, remembering my mission, even if he seems pleased under my scrutinizing gaze. "Yeah, I've missed hanging out. I've just been so busy."

He nods, staring out at the dark expanse of woods on the other side of his windshield. We're parked in his cop car at the far end of an abandoned parking lot near the Burger Blast. "I get it. We're so short-staffed at the station. That's why I could only meet up during my shift."

Perfect. He's bringing up work. Now, it won't seem weird when I question him. I reach over, running my long, red fingernails over the stubble on his head. He leans into it, closing his eyes. Ugh, men are so easy. They're like literal puppy dogs. All they need is for you to scratch their balls and fill their bellies, and they'll roll over.

"Why has the station been so busy? Anything unusual?" I lean closer so my breath tickles his ear. My questioning is a little on the nose—especially considering he knows I'm a reporter, but he's lost in my touch. He leans against the headrest, eyes closed, and lips parted. "Same old, same old," he replies.

Well, shit. I'm not here for same old, same old.

"Oh, boring," I say in a whiny tone. Maybe he'll offer more if he thinks it can impress me.

He chuckles. "I wouldn't say it's boring."

I lean in closer, crawling over the middle console so my rouged lips are near his ear. "Captured any psychopaths recently?"

His eyes open, and he turns to me, grabbing the back of my neck. "You girls always love to hear the exciting details."

Yes, perfect. I need him to think of me as a regular thrill-seeking girl. Honestly, he's probably forgotten that I'm a reporter, but I don't mind. Not in the slightest because now, hopefully, he won't have his guard up and will give me the information I'm searching for.

I lean my weight onto one elbow, bringing my other hand to his chest. He's wearing a thick vest, but I press hard, slowly lowering my hand. "What can I say? I could never do your job. Putting myself in the line of danger every day to defend the innocent? It's noble but scary. I bet it's so exciting, though." I might be laying on the act a little thick, but with my hand nearing his slacks, I bet the words seem like the perfect caress to his ego.

He shrugs, his eyes droop. "It has its exciting days, and it has its days like this, sitting alone in a cop car waiting for something to happen."

I trace the thick outline of his cock under his belt. He hisses. "Oh, so is this a boring day for you at the office?"

He smiles, his teeth white and straight. "This is an exception." His breath is heavy, and I toy with his outline. I can't deny I'm enjoying playing with him—watching him melt into my touch, all while wearing his uniform in a place I'm not supposed to be. Sure, I'm doing this for the greater good, but it doesn't hurt that Straw has a massive cock and a pretty face to look at while he breathes into me. "Oh, so you don't usually have women in your cop car?"

I mean it as a flirty probe, but Straw tenses, pulling away from my lips to study me. "I don't..."

I lay my hand on his chest. "I'm only joking."

His concern melts, and he smiles, a stupid, boyish, charming smile. I bet he's gotten away with murder with it. "Oh, okay." He leans in, pressing his lips against mine and pushing his tongue into me. It's sloppy and desperate, but I can't deny that it's nice. It's been a while since an attractive man has kissed me. I'm not here to make out with him. In fact, I explicitly told everyone I could get information without sleeping around, but I'm not the kind of girl to deprive myself of delicious man meat when it's thrown at me.

I kiss him back, my hand returning to his rock-hard body, trailing to the warm heat between his legs. He pulls away from my lips, spreading his legs wide and working at his belt buckle. The kissing didn't last long. I'd hope he'd touch me more before pulling his dick out, although the thought of blowing a cop in his patrol car sends a flush of liquid to my core that probably won't get attended to. Straw isn't the most generous lover, but I'm in a mood and a woman who loves gobbling some dick, even if I don't get the favor returned.

He springs free, hard and long, only visible from the light offered by the full moon. He brings his lips back to me, kissing me hungrily. I appreciate he doesn't just sit there and watch me until I feel so inclined to take him in my mouth. That always kills the mood. He's a fucking great kisser. He nips at my lips, tasting as if he doesn't care about displaying any reserve, as if he's so into this and doesn't mind showing it. It makes me eager to please, so I rub my palm over a dollop of the precum formed at his tip. He moans into my mouth as I roll my hand down his length, luxuriating in the feel of his velvety skin in my hand.

"Fuck, Carmen," he says, pulling away from my lips and resting his forehead against mine—his eyes clamp shut as if to restrain himself. It's hot—all of this. The fact that he could get in *so* much trouble if we were discovered only makes me wetter. Why haven't I tried to live out this fantasy sooner?

I pull away, leaning over his lap. He sits back, too ready to have my lips on his cock. I grab his base with one hand, and with the other, I find the heat underneath my skirt. I'm not embarrassed to get myself off. I'm slick, and my fingers slide through me easily. I moan over his dick before placing a soft kiss on his tip.

"Fuck, Carmen. You're always so good at this."

I haven't even started, but I appreciate the encouragement. I roll my lips over him, taking him in slowly to build the anticipation. He runs his hands through my hair, working his strong fingers against my scalp. I'd rather feel his fingers in my cunt, but this is nice too. I strum away at myself, circling my clit gently as I take him deeper.

"Oh, God," he moans with a hiss.

I work faster on both of us, bobbing up and down as his hold on my hair grows tighter, less scratching and more pulling. I fucking love it, actually. I rub my clit harder and faster, growing closer to my edge. A thought bubbles in my brain. Wasn't I here to find out about the kidnappings? Wouldn't it be a better idea to find out information before sucking his dick so I had something to tempt him with? Oops. I can't go back now.

I grab his balls, feeling them clench in my hand as I take him deeper. I slow my tempo as my orgasm washes over me, and I moan with his cock still deep in my mouth. He sputters into me, cum coating my throat. I flinch, shocked by the sudden burst. I thought that the break in tempo would have held him off more so I could prepare myself, but he must have gotten off from the sight of me coming with his dick in my mouth.

I sit up, making a disgusted face as I swallow his cum. It's warm, thick, and unpleasant tasting, but I swallow like a champ and wipe my mouth with the back of my hand. Thankfully, he's not paying attention to me. He works on stuffing himself back in his pants. "Fuck, it's always so hot that you get off from blowing me." He leans over and kisses my cheek.

He misses my scrunched expression. "Yeah, that's what happened." I chuckle.

His radio buzzes to life as if sent from the gods to erase an impending uncomfortable silence. "Dispatch, this is 543. Be advised, we have a possible 187 at a secluded residence off Pine Hollow Road, approximately 2 miles north of Route 47. Suspected murder victim inside the residence. Requesting immediate backup and crime scene unit. Proceed with caution. Over."

"Shit," Straw says, gritting his teeth.

My heart hammers, pulling my skirt down and taking in my surroundings outside the car. "Pine Hollow is right down the road."

"I'll take you home. Someone else will assist." He pulls the seatbelt over his chest.

"No bother, I want to go." I grab the door handle and swing it open. There's no chance he's driving me to the crime scene. I'll walk the five minutes before he has time to argue.

"Carmen, no!" he yells after me, but I'm already out of his car, slamming his door in his face. "I bet he remembers I'm a reporter now," I say to myself, rubbing at the thin material of my sweater as I walk to the dirt road ahead.

"Unit 5-Charlie-11 to Unit 2-Adam-12, I'm in the area and moving in on foot. Should be on scene in two minutes. Over."

I smile to myself as Straw runs up behind me, crunching the dead leaves underfoot. "Go back to the car and wait for me," he orders.

I turn around, walking backward and holding my wrists up. "What are you going to do? Arrest me?" I smirk. "I bet you'd love to see me in your handcuffs." I don't miss the way his pupils blow out from my words, even if his expression strains.

"You're going to get me in trouble," he grits through clenched teeth.

"You didn't seem to care too much about getting into trouble a few minutes ago." I wink and turn back around. "Don't worry. I won't say we came together. You should probably arrive in your patrol car to avoid making it look suspicious."

"I'm not going to let you walk through the woods by yourself to a murder crime scene. I don't know if they've caught the suspect." He sounds sincere and genuinely concerned for my safety. Cute. But more than that, I'm assuming he's unaware of the culprit in this murder. He's too dumb to lie well. The victim could be anyone, but I'm guessing it's a werewolf because the house is in a desolate area. I can't let the panic and sorrow overtake me yet. I must keep on with my cutesy, oblivious act until I see what has happened for myself. Maybe he doesn't know anything about the Hunters' plans, but there's no way to tell until I can watch him on the scene.

"You don't need to worry about me, Straw. I can take care of myself."

"Shit, you're fast." He grunts from behind me, trying to catch up with my strides. He's muscular, but I'm a werewolf, a fact he's unaware of. I could run laps around him, but I need to slow down not to make him suspicious. If he is working with the Hunters, he's not oblivious to our existence, and I don't want to make myself known.

Some of the police force knows about the Weres. Much like our Human Liaison, there's a similar status in the police force. It seems this title belongs to Brick now. Only he and a few stone-faced men under him know about our kind. I'm assuming Straw isn't high enough up at the station to be privy to my supernatural powers, but maybe he's just been playing dumb this whole time. I doubt it, but it would make him hotter if he were.

Emergency lights shine in the near distance. A house comes into view just a few steps down the hill. I don't recognize it, but it's not a surprise. Weres are secretive about their residence, even with their pack, and especially with the Human Liaison family. My racing heart can't take my pretend speed. I pick up my pace, not enough to raise suspicion, but leaving Straw behind me.

Only two police cars are parked out in the front. They weren't kidding when they said they needed backup, or maybe they don't want a big crowd here. A few other unmarked cars are in the driveway: an ambulance, a coroner, and perhaps family members' vehicles. I assess quickly, my eyes darting subtly as I march closer to the house's entrance. I can't bring attention to myself by gawking. I keep my gaze low, trying not to meet anyone's eyes. I nearly step over a fresh hoof print, but I don't stop to examine it. A horse whinnies nearby, and a police officer pats the mare's back. Okay, so there are police horses here. That doesn't mean anything to me yet.

I make my way inside, no one noticing my presence. I have no fucking idea where Straw is. Probably still stumbling down that hill. It helps that the crime scene is fresh and so few people are on location. No one has time to pay attention to me.

I gasp once I'm only a few steps into the house entryway, covering my mouth as I stare at Jessica's lifeless body on the rug parallel to the front door. It takes five seconds to take it all in: her slashed throat, her motionless eyes, the bloodied fingertips—Hunters did this, no doubt. Tears cloud my vision. I wasn't close to the girl. She was about five years my junior, but I always liked her. She reminded me of myself—never backing down, never staying quiet. I can't help but wonder if that's why she's here without a pulse instead of disappeared.

I scan around me, not missing the puddle of blood a few feet away from her. I'm hoping it belongs to the prick that did this to her. Although I'd much rather she be alive, a part of me revels in the fact that she fought and can only hope she made someone pay.

"What the fuck are you doing here?" A human wall steps before me, and a shadow looms overhead. My skin pricks at the sound of his voice. I know who it is immediately, but it still takes me two seconds to scan up the expanse of his broad body to meet his smokey grey eyes staring down at me. His ash brown hair differs from its usual well-kept combed-back look. It's loose and free and shows its true wavy texture. It takes two seconds to take in his unsettled energy. I just wonder the reason for his unease.

I swallow a knot in my throat and smile, pushing down my sorrow. "Brick, how ya' doing?"

His eyes blaze something furious, his hands clench at his side, a small notebook crushed as a result. "Carmen, what the fuck are you doing at my crime scene?" He scans me, reaching my short black skirt. He sucks in a sharp breath and clenches his eyes.

"Carm…" Straw trails from behind. I whip to the doorway to see him out of breath, eyes wide as he catches Brick staring him down over the top of my head. I turn back to Brick, his jaw twitching under his strain as he holds Officer Straw in place with his murderous gaze.

Blood and gore surround me, but I can't help but smile at Brick's obvious unease. I cross my arms over my chest. "Brick, I was…" I don't finish my sentence. Brick grabs my arm and yanks me out the front door, pushing past Straw. "Fucking take evidence pictures. Don't leave before we speak," Brick yells at Straw as he points one massive finger in his direction, his other hand probably leaving marks on my forearm.

I can't find a reaction to the sudden assault until I'm out in the cool night air, moonlight shining overhead. Brick releases me and I rub at the sore spot. "What the fuck?" Anger finds its footing in my veins.

Brick crouches to my eye level, now wielding the monstrous finger at me. "No, explain why you are here."

Letting my lashes lower, I deliver a searing look. Sure, Brick is always a prick, especially to me for some reason, but he's never touched me and usually shows his distaste with a huff and an eye roll. He's fuming, staring at me as if I'm his petulant child who nearly ran into the road. It makes me all the more suspicious of him. Maybe I just caught him red-handed, and he's shitting bricks thinking he's about to get caught. Ha ha. Brick shitting bricks.

I cross my arms, taking a calming breath, not missing the twitch at his temple as if my ease upsets him further. "I work for the public, Bricky. It's my duty to investigate for the public's interest."

He shakes his head, clenching his jaw tighter. "No, you're in the way. We need to collect evidence without the presence of the public." He steps closer, lowering his lips to my ear. His words strain through his teeth. "Don't you want justice for her? Don't let the murder of one of your own end in a mistrial."

I step away from him. The heat of his body already soaking into mine, roasting my insides. "I didn't plan to touch anything!" I yell.

He ignores me, cornering me further. "Tell me how you knew about this so quickly."

His eyes hold me in accusation. Does he think I have inside information about this murder? That I could know who did it? It would be stupid of him to assume that. He knows from my years of bugging him in his office to get his ass working on bringing my people justice where my loyalty lies. But just to make sure, I offer him the truth. "I was with Straw when it came over his radio." Sorry, Straw, but greater good and all.

My revelation makes him anything but calmer. "With Straw? Doing what?" He nearly backs me into a tree.

I push him away from me, using my wolf strength to propel him an impressive distance. He may be a foot taller than me, but I'm a werewolf. He can't make me feel small unless I let him. It's like he'd forgotten what I was for a moment because his eyes widen a tiny bit as he regains his footing. But the heat and fury only take seconds to return to his pupils, and he steps closer again. At least this time, giving me a breath of room. "Are your officers not allowed to be in the presence of their citizens, Sergeant?"

"Carmen, this wouldn't be the first time you distracted my men from their jobs."

My mind plays back to the few instances Officer Straw and Wood came in handy for me when I needed information on a story. There was also that one time I fucked Wood in the coat closet at the country club in his uniform, and a few people witnessed us coming out together. I bet that got back to Brick somehow. Considering both men still have jobs, I guess it wasn't too much of an issue for Brick. Or Brick has some dirty secrets he doesn't want to get out. The latter seems the most likely.

"Jealous?" I taunt, twisting my lips in a smirk.

It's the wrong thing to say. Brick grabs my wrist, twisting me around and bringing both arms behind my back.

"What the fuck!" I yell as he snaps handcuffs on me. "Are you on your period or something? You can't be for real." I struggle, exerting my *real* strength, but it's futile. Brick overpowers me. We've always suspected Brick was something other than human, but even as I sniff him now, I can't catch a whiff of wolf. It's ridiculous. We've revealed the fragile identities of our people, and yet we don't even know who he is. Our mission to end Hunters' cruelty supersedes the unknown of Brick's origins, and up until this point, our pack thought he was on our side. Now that I'm restrained and he's pushing me deeper into the woods, I realize just how wrong my people's trust was placed.

"Brick, where the fuck are you taking me?"

He doesn't answer; he just keeps pushing me along until we're covered by an expanse of trees and completely out of sight. Shit, maybe I'm the next victim of these strings of Hunter murders.

He whips me around, flinging the air from my lungs. His chest grazes my own, and his grey eyes change to charcoal. I'm unsure if it's the absence of light in the woods, the moon barely providing any illumination, or if his irises change to match his mood. It seems I know shit about Brick, and these puddles of black might be the last things I see.

His face is a mask of stone. When the words slip from his mouth, I nearly scream, the sound surprising me. "No more messing with my officers. You want information; you come to me."

Barricaded breath escapes from me. Okay, he's ordering me around as if I'll have a tomorrow. It makes me want to punch him across the jaw, but at least I don't think he's planning to kill me.

I decide to test my luck further. "You and I both know you never tell me anything. In fact, you always send me away without even listening to my question."

He takes in a deep breath. "We don't get along. That's obvious. You aren't a lone agent. You have a pack. If *they* want answers, *they* can send your brother to ask them."

I give a pained smile. "My brother's a little busy."

"Then they can send someone else."

God, this man hates me. I fucking hate him, too, but his distaste for me is the reason that's so. It only makes me more suspicious of him. There's an energy about him—a buzz that sets my balance off kilter. He's not the man he's portraying to be. My instincts scream the truth, but I won't get anywhere with him now. "Are you arresting me?"

My words startle him just the slightest, and his gaze moves away from my eyes and down my body as if just remembering he put me in handcuffs.

He turns me around and unlocks my chains, but before I'm free, he lowers his head to the shell of my ear. "Not this time, but I mean it. No more fraterniz-ing with my officers. Leave the police work to me and tell Grimm to come to me with questions."

I can't tell him the truth—that Grimm and the rest of our pack don't trust him anymore and that I'm not going to back down and wait for him and the Hunters to murder the rest of our pack. He's more dangerous than I initially thought. Now, I need to get the fuck away from him and seek out my other source. The fact that Brick doesn't want me near his men only confirms my suspicion that one of them knows something. Straw seems useless—either oblivious to what's happening or so well trained that he won't give it up, but Wood still could be helpful.

My plans run through my mind, but the reality of the situation just steps away washes over me. Jessica is dead. One more of us is gone, and we have failed to protect her. I take a deep breath to ground my sorrow, still facing away from Brick, I clamp my eyes shut. "Why was she killed?" I ask, my voice wobbly.

He sighs, silent for a moment as if considering to divulge me. "It looks like an abduction gone wrong."

"Like the last one?"

He turns me around, studying me, not getting any further away. "Carmen, you don't like me, but I need you to trust me. Lie low. Stay away. Let me take care of this." I can usually tell when people are lying. I can hear their heartbeats speed up, feel their pulse heighten in their veins, and watch as their eyes dart and give them away. As Brick stares down at me, close enough to sense every minuscule movement under his skin, I can't sense any unease. He appears to be telling the truth, as he honestly believes I should trust him. But I can't believe my senses with him. He's obviously not human or werewolf. He goes against everything I know about the world.

"Okay," I say, hoping he can't sniff out the lie in me.

He nods, stepping away, and the air lightens immediately. I study him for one final second before I shift. My clothes drop to the forest floor around me, and I shake my black fur free. Brick isn't alarmed at my transformation. I've never shifted in front of him and wonder if any of the other Weres have. There's nothing to hide and I want to remind him what I am. I'm not just a small woman who can be easily bent. I'm a monster, a force to be reckoned with. Even if he is something else, I've faced much worse.

I sprint away from Brick and the carnage. As I get farther and farther away, my questions grow. But damn it if I'm not selfish and frivolous because all I keep thinking about is that I really liked that shirt I was wearing, and now I'm never going to get it back.

4

MEN ARE PIGS

Two fake dates in two nights can make a girl feel one of two ways, either like a sexy international spy seducing foreign threats to their demise or like something a little more desperate. I take another sip of my fruity cocktail so the alcohol can melt my image of myself as the latter.

"I'm so glad you texted," Wood says, leaning into his palm propped up on the sticky bar counter.

My eyes assess him over the rim of my cocktail glass. He's less handsome than I remember. Sure, he's muscular with dark hair and thick eyebrows, but his eyes dart all over, as if he'd rather be in a million other places. I can't tell if it's my werewolf senses kicking or if it's obvious to a regular human, but there's something untrustworthy about him, something that makes me squirm in my seat. But I'm not here to decide if I like him or even have a nice evening. I'm here to find out what he knows.

After leaving the crime scene last night, I notified Cameron and Grimm about Jessica's murder. I prepared for a late-night council meeting to discuss the tragic events with the pack, but they suggested we hold off until he had anything that could offer them hope. Thanks to the Hunters' past attacks, Jessica had no family and didn't attend the last council meeting. Cameron said he'd work on ensuring all the young women in our pack knew the importance of staying with others. Besides that, they didn't want to alarm the pack further, not until I had this date and found out something—anything.

I also informed the males of Brick's suspicious nature. They didn't say much; they just listened. They seemed comforted when I told them he told me to trust him, but they still had their guards up, as they should. For me, I had a whole militia armed around my trust in that man.

I flash a smile, setting my half-drunk drink on the bar. "I've missed you." I bat my eyelashes and push forward on my crossed arms, hoping my breasts spill out of my low-cut top.

Sure enough, his eyes travel straight to my trap. He stares at my tits for longer than acceptable. Yes, I offered them up to him, but you'd think he'd have the decency to play coy. This will be too easy.

He *finally* brings his eyes back to mine before grabbing my bar chair and pulling it to his. To his credit, he moves me and my chair as if we were weightless. I mean, I could do the same thing to him, but still, I like a strong man. Definitely not this man, but as the alcohol swims through my veins, he's growing on me. His lips are inches away from mine, but instead of removing the distance, he yells to the bartender, "Let's get another round over here."

I smile, contemplating if I should drink more or keep my wits about myself. But as Wood strains in an attempt to show off his biceps, I decide this will be insufferable without one or two more drinks.

Those one or two drinks turn into about five. I'm usually pretty good at restraining myself, but Wood keeps ordering them, and I'm not one to turn down anything free. Before I know it, my head spins, and the edges of reality are light and fluffy. By the grace of some divine entity, I remember the seeds of my mission. I take a small sip of my martini, splashing a bit as I set it on the counter, sticky from the likes of me. "Wood."

"I told you, call me John."

I roll my eyes, laugh, and push his shoulder. "Fineee! Okay, John. I have a question." I hiccup.

Our stools are touching, and I'm nearly seated on his lap. He runs his hands lower down my back, nearly slipping into the hem of my skirt and grabbing my ass. I notice it slightly, but everything is just too funny right now to care. "Tell me, have you ever seen a dead body?" It's a stupid question. I know that even as I'm clearly drunk, even in my inebriated state, I have a line of questions set up and ready to take a domino effect.

He shakes his head, smiling at me as if I'm an airhead. It annoys me even with the alcohol. "Yes. I've seen a dead body."

I lean in, bringing my lips to his ear. "Did you see the body of that girl who died last night?" I pull back, pretending to look terrified.

He twists his lips, "No, I was across town. I heard it was pretty gruesome."

"Who do you think did it?" I take another sip of my drink, willing myself to sober up to gauge if he's lying. Sadly, my powers don't work as well with alcohol, something I hope a Hunter never discovers. It's not a side effect for all Weres, but it's definitely one for me. Of course, perfect Cameron can drink a whole barrel of wine and not even lose a minuscule of his strength.

Wood motions me closer with his finger, and I comply. His breath smells wheaty from his beer. "I think it's just an old boyfriend. It was a young girl. That's usually the MO."

"But there was a girl who just died similarly a few days ago. Do you think it could be a serial killer?"

He eyes me quizzically. "You seem to know a lot about these murders." He says it so clearly. I eye his drink resting on the bar, realizing it's still mostly full. I try to remember how many he got for himself, but honestly, my memory is shit right now. I adjust myself in my seat, my legs and leather skirt sticking to the faux leather of the stool. I push his shoulder playfully. "Josh, I'm a reporter, silly. Remember."

"It's John." His expression sags.

"I knew that." I laugh, rubbing my hand down my face, hoping I'm not smearing my make-up. I'm just drunk."

He shakes his head with a sigh. "Why don't we get you home?"

I want to protest. I haven't discovered anything about what Wood knows, but my investigative skills aren't up to par right now. In fact, a toddler would be better at investigating things. I decide it's best to cut my losses and call it a night. Maybe I can count this as a buttering-up session. Wood's not getting anything tonight, and maybe I turned him on a bit. He'll want to see me again to seal the deal.

I throw my weight into him, and luckily, he catches me, directing my feet to the ground. He laughs. "Woah, let's get out of here."

I nod and follow him out of the smoky bar, past the patrons playing pool. The cool night air slaps against my face as we exit. Thankfully, my drunkenness makes the chill stinging my bare legs less painful. I intertwine my arm with Wood's, using him as support as we walk down the sidewalk. I took an Uber here and would likely take one back, but my house isn't too far away. Wood's been to my place before, so he knows the way. I'm one of the few werewolves who live closer to the town and not in a cabin in the woods. Everyone already knows who I am, so there's no point hiding.

Time moves quickly. Wood stops walking straight and turns down an unlit alley. "Where are we going?" I ask, my eyes growing heavy.

"Shortcut," he replies.

I accept it momentarily, but then he steps and pushes me against the brick wall. His hands run down my front, and his lips crash against mine. The surprise sobers me up a bit, and I close my mouth, turn my head, and push him away. "Come on, Wood. Not now. I'm too drunk."

"Don't be a buzzkill," he whispers into my ear, his hands returning to my breasts. "You look sober enough to blow me."

No amount of alcohol can mask the ick his words just gave me. I push him again, channeling an ounce of my werewolf strength to get my point across. But even as reality settles over me, I'm still wasted. I'm weak, my powers muted. Shit. "Wood. No. We can hook up another time. Let's schedule something for next week." I'm never seeing this pig again, but I'm no idiot. I need to get out of here.

He presses closer, crushing me a little bit, and brings his lips to my ears. "Straw told me you gave him head in his patrol car. You didn't even ask for anything in return, just got yourself off like a good little slut. I want that, too."

My heart races and panic swims through me. I've never felt this feeling before, weak, helpless. Sure, I've been drunk and without powers, but never while being cornered by a man who insists on taking what isn't his.

I try one last time, adding air to my voice. "Let's do this back at my place. It's too cold."

His hands travel up my thigh. "I'll keep you warm." He brings his mouth to mine again. Fuck being coy to get out of this. I bite his lip, hard. I'm pretty sure a fang makes it through. He shrieks, grabbing his face, and I use the opportunity to push him away and sprint in the opposite direction. Trash litters the walkway, and I barely make it a few feet before my foot snags a discarded box, and I tumble to the ground with a scream. I'm pathetic without my powers.

Pain shoots from the knee that took the brunt of the fall. I'm distracted, and as I claw to make my way back to my feet, Wood pushes my back down with his foot.

"Why are you being such a bitch?" He grits angrily.

"A bitch? You're trying to rape me, jackass!" I yell, hoping someone, anyone, will hear. He drops to his knees, flipping me to my back and covering his hand with my mouth. He glowers over me. "Don't yell shit like that. Are you playing a game with me?"

I try to tell him no, that if I wanted to fuck him, I'd tell him, but all that comes out is a muffled scream from under his hand. A question pops into my drunk mind, and I use all my strength to wiggle my mouth free to ask it. "Did you do this to Jessica and Lucy? Was it you who murdered them because they wouldn't fuck you?" I know it was the Hunters, but maybe Wood is working for them and wanted some action on the spot.

His face changes to repulsion. "What? No! I'm not a murderer, and I'm not a rapist. I've never met those girls in my life. I'm not raping you. You've sucked my dick plenty of times. You're just playing a game."

I steady my voice. "John, no, I am not. I do not want you anywhere near me." I say the words as if I'm saying them to a child, or a man who has never heard the word no in his life.

"Hey, what's going on here?" It could be the words from the goddamn devil, and I would worship at his feet. A question has never sounded so beautiful. "This jackass is trying to rape me!" I shout.

"Woah, woah, woah." Wood jumps to his feet and steps away from me, his hands raised in surrender. "Carmen, stop it." He diverts his attention to the man walking toward us. "We're just role-playing. We've hooked up plenty of times before."

I grunt, climbing to my feet. "Fuck that! You were trying to rape me, you fucking piece of shit." I straighten out my skirt and shirt before turning to my savior.

"From my vantage point, it sure looked like you were attacking her." I notice the accent, and my attention is drawn to the blonde, muscular man now standing mere feet from me. Our eyes lock, and I'm too stunned to speak. "Carmen?" he gets out breathlessly.

I nod, clenching my lips. "And that's the cop."

The confusion melts off his face, fury in its place. He moves past me, rushing toward Wood and punching him across the jaw, knocking him to the floor.

"What the fuck?" Wood spits, his lip bleeding even more now.

Kilo drops to a squat. "You fucking come near her again, and I'll end you." The lights in the alleyway are low, so I barely make out the subtle shift in Kilo. His black sweater tightens, ripping at the bottom, and snow-white hair juts from the back of his neck and arms. He doesn't lose control, keeping his transformation at bay.

"What? Is she your girl or something? Sorry to tell you, but you're dating a slut."

Kilo chuckles, shaking his head and turning to me. "Do you hear this guy?" he asks me. "It's like he wants to get fucking killed." It happens so quickly. He pounces on top of Wood, revealing claws and fangs. He growls, and Wood cries in terror from underneath him. "What the fuck?" he yells.

Kilo switches back to his complete human form. To someone who didn't know what he was, they'd think they just imagined the shift; it happened so quickly.

"Do you need any more convincing how easy I could make you die?"

"Okay, got it!" Wood's crying now, a blubbering mess. It's the best thing I have ever seen, and I have half the mind to pull out my phone and record this, but I resist the urge, for Kilo's sake.

Kilo doesn't move. "Now, apologize to the lady, and you better make it good."

"I'm sorry. I'm so sorry." He boo-hoo cries as if this is years of pent-up sorrow. I can't suppress my chuckle.

Kilo turns to me. "What do you think?"

I shrug. "It'll do."

"You sure? I could bite a finger off for good measure."

"Tempting, but I just want to go home at this point." I love the display of justice before me, but I need a bubble bath. I'm filthy, cold, and annoyed.

Kilo pops to his feet. "Let's go." He intertwines his arm with mine and leads me out of the dirty hallway. "You okay?" he asks, examining me.

"Yeah. I'm fine."

We walk in silence down the cobblestone street, and I breathe in the fresh air, my mind replaying everything that just happened. Thankfully, my knee only slightly hurts. Fuck, that was scary. New rule: no more drinking with men I don't trust with my life. It should have already been a rule, but it never worried me until now. I guess you don't know what to worry about until it happens.

"Want to talk about it?" Kilo asks once several minutes of silence have passed.

I sigh, pushing my hair out of my face. "Not really."

"Got it." He stares straight ahead, still holding my arm and walking at a comfortable speed. I pull him as we reach a corner toward my house. He's silent, heading my request and not pressing more. I kind of hate it. "I just want to say I haven't slept with that guy in months, okay?"

He gives me a disapproving look. "Don't defend yourself. I don't hold a word that pig says to any sort of value."

"I know, I know. I just wanted to make that clear. I feel like you've known me for all of two seconds, and the only information you've heard about me is about my ability to sleep around. I'm a fantastic lay, but I'm much more than that, okay?"

He chuckles, the sound foreign after the events of the night. "You're right. I have known you for a very short time, and I can already tell you are so much more than I think you're even aware of."

My cheeks burn, and I can't help but smile. The compliment is nice, cheesy, but so wonderful after being pushed face-down in a dirty alleyway and nearly being taken advantage of. I can't even find the words to express my gratitude to him, so instead, I kiss him on the cheek.

He flips his gaze to me, eyes wide, and a smile slowly creeps up his face. It's a nice smile—bright, white, and genuine. "Thank you," I say.

"For what?"

I laugh. "For what? You just saved me, and now being way too nice, and I barely even know you."

"We're both Weres. We have to stick together. And maybe your irresistible charm and uncanny good looks have something to do with it, too."

I bark a laugh. "Oh, so if I had a boil, you'd have left me for dead."

"No! But I probably wouldn't let you snuggle up to me on your walk home and tell you how beautiful you are." My damn cheeks heat again. I pull back a bit, realizing I am, in fact, cuddling up to him. It's fucking cold, and he also smells nice and feels nice. Besides, I'm still a little drunk, which reminds me, "By the way! I'm usually pretty fucking powerful! I could have taken that dick with my eyes closed if my brain wasn't inebriated."

He laughs. "I know. You don't have to tell me you're drunk. I can tell."

"You can not tell! I'm so good at acting sober." I walk in front of him, doing a twirl before nearly tripping and falling to my ass. He rushes to my side, pulling me up at the last second. I laugh at myself for making this guy save me yet again. "Okay, maybe I should just shut up and stop."

"You're fine. You should be allowed to drink. Men should be here to care for you, not hurt you."

"I can take care of myself, thank you very much." It's a stupid thing to say because, obviously not.

"I know you can, most of the time, but everyone needs someone sometimes."

"True. Like those girls need me." The reality of the horrifying events settles around me. I'm going to need another drink to forget their lifeless eyes. There are still three girls that need my help.

"I know it's a bad time to ask, but did you discover anything?"

I shake my head. "Honestly, I don't think he knows anything. I mean, I'm drunk, so I'm probably not the sharpest with picking up intuitions, but I accused him of killing the girls when he was about to assault me. He seemed genuinely confused. You'd think he wouldn't need to hide it when he was about to do something horrible anyway."

Kilo hums in agreement. We pass a busy, well, busy for Dayton, intersection. Shop lights twinkle from all sides of us. I'm almost home, just one more block, thank God. But God must not be too happy with me because even drunk, beat up, and distracted, I can't miss him.

Brick is pressed against a building parallel to us, hidden by the shadows but more than visible to me. He's in a deep conversation with someone. We pass him, and thankfully, he misses me. I turn around to see who he was talking to. It's Richard Wilson; his handlebar mustache makes him impossible to mistake. He was the second in command when Jack Lumberton was in power as the Hunters' leader. Now that Jack is dead, thanks to Red and Cameron, it only makes sense that Richard would take his place.

Kilo must sense my body stiffen. "What is it?" he asks, out of earshot of the two men.

"I just saw Brick."

"Brick?"

"The cop that was supposed to be on our side. He was talking to a Hunter, the lead Hunter."

Kilo whips his head around, but they're probably only specks behind us now. "Did it look like a cordial conversation?"

"Much too cordial for my liking."

"So he is working with the Hunters?"

"It would seem so."

"Did he see us?"

I shrug. "I don't think so." I sigh. There is so much to debrief with Grimm tomorrow. I'm already exhausted. My house comes into view, and I stop. I should be weary of men after the night I just had, but Kilo did save me. It's probably not an issue that he knows where I live. "Well, this is me."

"Are you going to be alright?"

"Thanks to you."

He smiles. It's so cute. I can't help it. I lean in, kissing him square on the mouth. He stiffens in surprise but parts his lips and kisses me back. It only lasts a moment before he pushes me away, laughing. "Alright, why don't you go to bed, and if you still want to kiss me tomorrow, give me a call." My cheeks heat. Shit. What the fuck was I doing? I just tried to convince him I wasn't a slut like Wood implied, and now here I am, kissing him like I can't control myself. I sigh. "It's the alcohol."

He laughs. "I know. Have a good night."

I throw my head back. "Thanks again. Sorry for kissing you." I walk toward my front door.

"Don't be sorry!" he yells. "Just save it for later." I turn around just in time to see him wink.

Surprisingly, I make it into my house with a smile. After everything that happened tonight, you'd think I'd be in tears, but it makes me happy to know all men aren't pigs.

5

PIGGY PROBLEMS

I steady my footsteps as the mountainside comes into view. One of the good things about meeting at the cave is that I can arrive in my human form and clothes. With my hangover this morning, shifting would have hurt like a bitch. I would deserve it, though. I was drunk last night, but clearly, I wasn't drunk enough because I remember *everything*, at least I think I do, and I'm horrified at myself. I'm not going to take the blame for Wood's monstrous actions, but I can't believe I let my guard down completely when I planned to investigate if Wood was covering up the Hunters' murders. I shouldn't have trusted him enough to drink alone with him, but I guess since I'd been with him, alone, so many times before, I had a false sense of security. Like yeah, maybe he's kidnapping women, but he wouldn't do that to *me*. I'm an idiot.

And then there was the whole Kilo situation. I can't believe I kissed him after everything he just saved me from. Sure, he's good-looking, but I don't know if I would have been so ready to fall into his arms without encouragement from my previous martinis. He called me beautiful and told me all these sweet, sappy things, and now I've led him on. I have enough men in my life causing havoc. I don't need another, even if he seems like a good guy.

From now on, I'll do whatever it takes to find out where the missing women are. I owe it to them. I've already spent enough time dicking around.

Kilo must have spilled the beans to Grimm because, low and behold, my phone rang off the hook bright and early at eight fucking am. Grimm's low voice scraped against my tender brain, informing me we must meet at the caves in an hour before abruptly hanging up. I didn't have time to grumble and request more time.

Now, here I am before the inconspicuous wall of stone. I tap on a section three times. To someone who doesn't know, it looks like a regular section of a mountain wall covered in vines, but if you were to look very closely, you'd make out the subtle outline. The door swings open, and Jeremy, Grimm's nephew, steps into view.

"How ya' doing kid?" I ask as I enter the cool cave, and he closes the door behind me.

"Shit," he replies.

I spurt a laugh. "Why?"

"My uncle is making me do all this random work. Filing papers, cleaning his office, this is supposed to be my summer break, and he's ruining it." We walk side by side down the stone walkway, lanterns adhering to the walls illuminating our path.

"Sorry to hear that, but hey, maybe you can put the work on your resume."

He gives me a disgruntled look. "I'm going to college next year. I can't say I worked for the Werewolf Minister on my applications."

"Maybe leave the werewolf part out, but you can definitely say you did office admin work. I bet Grimm would vouch for you if you needed a reference."

He shrugs. "I guess. I'm just glad school starts in a month, and I'm free of his reign. He's a hard ass."

I laugh, squinting as I try to picture Grimm ordering people around. Sure, he's a great leader and a commanding man, but I've never actually seen him tell anyone to do something. Maybe it's different with family. I know it sure is for me. Speaking of family, we near a corner, and Grimm's office comes into view. Cameron and Kilo are seated on the opposite side of Grimm's desk.

I sigh. "Well, good luck, kid, and wish me luck." He nods, his fingers around the doorframe before turning and sauntering down the hallway.

"Wait, Jeremy, before you go!" Grimm calls from his desk. Grimm doesn't see it, but upon hearing his voice, Jeremy sprints down the stone walkway, away from the office.

"Ah, you missed him," I say, entering and suppressing my giggle.

Grimm runs his large hands through his thick salt and pepper hair—heavy on the salt, low on the pepper. He grumbles. "My sister spoiled that kid. He doesn't want to show an ounce of hard work, and I'm doing his mom a favor by occupying him this summer so he doesn't get in trouble."

I pull out the wooden seat between Cameron and Kilo, sitting and pushing myself closer to the desk. "Summer's almost over, then he'll be out of your hair," I offer, thankful for the opportunity not to have to focus on my epic fail from the night before for a few moments.

He huffs. "Yeah, but then I'll actually need to find a secretary. Let me know if you think of anyone."

"Will do," I reply, staring straight ahead. I don't want to catch whatever smug expression my brother has on his face or get confused in Kilo's eyes.

Someone's a little impatient, though. "So, what happened?" Cameron asks, leaning forward and stealing my attention.

"Kilo didn't tell you?" I shoot the blonde a look.

"It's not my story to tell," he replies with a humble shrug.

"Wait. You were there?" Cameron slides up in his chair, glaring at Kilo from my other side.

"I wasn't there for all of it."

Cameron gives him a scrunched-face look. "You could have told us. Weird to just not say anything when we were making our predictions of what happened."

Cameron's being a dick. It's odd since he seemed so chummy with Kilo on the council meeting day, but it's probably just the effect of Red being so close to her due date.

I rest my hand on Kilo's thigh. "Well, I, for one, appreciate the discretion. Thank you, Kilo." I smile at him, and his cheeks blush. I pull my hand away, remembering my lips on his just hours before.

"Okay? So what fucking happened then?" Cameron barks.

I sigh. Where do I start? I'm thankful Kilo didn't reveal things without me present, but now I have to relive the events and admit to everyone here how much of a failure I am. Of course, I want to shout to the rooftops that Wood is a rapist and should be put behind bars, or six feet under the ground, but I can save that for another article. Right now, we need to find those girls before it's too late and stop more girls from going missing.

"I'll skip the minor details. Basically, I don't think Wood knows anything."

Cameron parts his lips, an angry syllable about to escape, but I stop him, already knowing what he's going to say. "No, I'm not sure, but I am sure about something."

"What?" He sighs, clearly impatient with my already very spark-notes story.

I shoot him a glare. "Chill, daddy grouchy pants." Sick burn, I know.

He laughs at that, and my spirits rise the tiniest bit that I can still make my deranged brother smile. "I saw Brick talking to Richard Wilson."

Cameron and Grimm both sit forward in their seats. "Where did you see them? Did they see you?" Grimm asks.

"I saw them while I was walking down Main Street. It was dark and pretty busy, but they were on the other side of the road, and they didn't see me."

"Are you sure?" Cameron asks before I can stop him this time.

I grit my teeth. "No, but he didn't stop talking to him or make it look like an altercation instead, so I'm willing to bet on it."

"Fuck!" Cameron falls back into his seat. "He's two-timing us, and he knows all the identities of our pack."

Grimm sighs. "We knew this was possible, but I think this just confirms it."

"Alright." Cameron's defeat is short-lived. "Let's get a group together and get him, interrogate him until he reveals the girls' locations."

"I don't think that's the best course of action," Kilo replies from next to me. Cameron shoots him a glare. Man, someone's on my brother's shit list this morning. I wonder if he knows we kissed, and this is some weird older brother protection thing going on. Cameron can sense things about others, but he's never been the overbearing type before. Maybe it's another effect of the baby.

"I agree," Grimm says, cutting the growing tension. "If Brick really is a double agent, he'll be much too skilled to reveal anything in an interrogation, and I'm not willing to break the humanity we've spent centuries working for by using torture."

Cameron grunts and falls back in his seat, crossing his arms. "Well, we need to think of something. We can't just follow him around until he fucks up. We need something faster than that." I study his profile, noticing the thin lines of grey coming from his scalp. Dark circles underline his eyes. This is killing him. His pack is in danger, and he's about to bring a baby into a perilous world. I can't let him carry the burden of this. I have to do something to fix this.

"I can go undercover." The words pass my lips before I know what I'm saying.

"What?" Cameron says, turning to me.

"I've already offered my skills of seduction with Straw and Wood, and that proved to be worthless." I shrug. "It's obviously one of my most impressive skills, so I should use it to actually help."

"Carmen," Grimm says in a concerned tone.

"I don't think that's a good idea. We don't want a recap of last time," Kilo says.

I whip my attention to him. Moments ago, he was all about preserving my dignity, and now he's so willing to give up the information.

"What do you mean last time? You met her like two fucking days ago?" Cameron barks.

I shake my head, holding my hands in front of both males. "It's fine. I had a slip of judgment last night with Wood. I truly don't think he has anything to do with the Hunters, but he's still a piece of shit. Kilo was there to intervene. I can handle this." Even as I say the words, my stomach flips.

I can barely be in the presence of Brick for more than five seconds without my blood pressure spiking. He loathes me. In fact, he told me that he wanted the council to send anyone besides me to converse with him. Do I really think I can seduce the man? Why do I even want to? But I know why.

Ever since I was a little girl and knew my brother had the life-long task of protecting our people, I've felt guilty. His life was constantly on the line while I shared the same DNA and escaped from any sort of responsibility. I've watched the strain on him. I've witnessed it almost crush him to a pulp. Now he has so much more: a wife who I adore and a child on the way that I already love with my whole being. Even if that wasn't enough, I care for those young women. They are part of me, and I've vowed to use my voice to protect them. I've failed. Over the past few days, I've tried to help, but I've come up short, and my failings are all my fault. I thought with my vagina before thinking with my brain. This is my chance to redeem myself. I'm hot, and I'm not afraid to admit it. Maybe Brick hates me now, but I can change that. In fact, now that a moral good is tied to it, I'm thrilled to see myself victorious. I can't wait to make him fall to his knees before me and slice off his balls. Metaphorically, of course. Well, maybe. If he's as evil as I think, it would be nice to do some villain testicle chopping.

"You don't have to do this, Carmen. I know you think I implied you use promiscuity to get info on the officers, but I would never put you in that situation," Grimm says from behind his desk, leaning forward and folding his hands.

"Yeah, I don't like this idea at all," Kilo says from my side. Strike two, Kilo. I turn to him, catching genuine concern riddling the lines of his features. Shit, I really affected this guy. I wonder what the women are like in Norway if he's so smitten after the less-than-desirable traits I've displayed over the past couple of days.

I place my hand on his knee. "Don't worry about me. I know you haven't seen an accurate example of my strength, but I promise to stay completely sober during this mission. I can take Brick if need be." I try to stuff away the memory of Brick overpowering me completely sober at the crime scene. That had to be a flux. I can handle this.

"Yeah, my sister can take care of herself."

"Thanks, bro." I pat his leg, scrunching my brow in confusion. What did Kilo do to him? Maybe he hates Norwegians or something and just discovered his origins.

Grimm sighs. "Cameron's right. She's one of our most powerful. I'd want her at the front line even if I weren't under these circumstances. As long as you are completely okay with the implications of this mission, I think it's a good idea."

"I can do this." But even as I say the words, a rotten plum falls to the base of my stomach. No one knows what Brick is. We're not addressing his otherness; maybe it's better this way. Maybe if we pretend he's just a normal man or even has a low strand of werewolf in him, we can overtake him and save these women. Even if he wasn't powerful, this man hates me. One thing is for certain, I'm about to pop my pussy like it's my superpower.

6

PIG SKIRT

A cool breeze blows through the sea glass wind-chime hanging from the banister of my porch. There's no sea glass in Dayton. I got it on my trip to the Keys in high school. It's a subtle reminder that there's more out there than Dayton. I've left this place and could do it again. Right now, I want to pack up my car and hit the road, abandoning my problems and not having to compose this email. It's just an email. I've killed people before, but this task seems more daunting than ripping out a throat.

I sigh, throwing my head back against the porch swing, staring up at the Douglas fir branches shading the front of my single-story craftsman home. I love my place. It's small but just enough room for a single person. When I bought it five years ago, it could have been a shit hole inside. The porch sold me before even stepping through the door. The inside did actually need a ton of work, but I had help from my pack to clean it up.

Whenever one of the Weres gets close to me or stops by my house, they risk their safety. My identity has never been hidden, while most of them spent their lives hiding their true selves. Sometimes, I pity myself for growing up in so much danger while simultaneously hiding in my brother's shadow, but I always know there's a threat. I'm never wondering if people will discover me. They have to live, stepping around caution, and yet still, some of them get murdered or kidnapped. It's a guilt I don't think will ever leave me, but I hope one day it does, maybe if I can save these girls.

My focus sharpens, and I look back down at my phone. I've spent the last half hour just staring at the white block in my email app—the *to* line already filled out. Fuck it. I type quickly, not rereading before hitting send. Once it's too late to second-guess myself, I reread.

Brick, can we meet? -Carmen

Perfect. Short, sweet, to the point, and will leave him with a dose of intrigue. Now, I just have to wait until he replies. It's a Sunday, and it's his work email I got from the county website, so I mentally prepare myself not to receive anything today. I vow not to continue glancing at my phone and actually get a handle on the clean laundry piles overtaking my room.

My phone dings. It's from him. I click the new notification. His response is even shorter but a lot less sweet. *No.*

I nearly throw my phone into my front yard. That asshole. Before thinking my fingers move furiously, composing a response. *Why?* Send.

I expect a quick response this time, but honestly, he'll probably ghost me. That seems more like him, but the email comes through just a few minutes later.

What is this in relation to? Avoiding my question. Nice.

Don't think it's a good idea to disclose through an email that's public record.

Send someone else.

There is no one else. It seems against the laws of emailing that we're responding this fast to each other.

I know that's not true. I think for a moment. He's right. We could send Grimm, Kilo, or even my brother, but they don't have tits to distract him with. A thought pops into my head. Why am I so certain that he'd be distracted by tits? Honestly, I pray he's gay. Then, the task can disappear from my consciousness, and I can throw up my hands and say I tried my best, at least in this aspect. But I have a feeling he isn't gay. The way he assesses me always leaves me feeling bare. He hates me too much to fuck me, at least as of right now, but I know he's thought about it. I could get him. Maybe it's overconfidence. Maybe I'm just intrigued by the challenge. I'm not sure, but I must see this through. So far, I've done nothing to help, and this feels like something I can handle—maybe.

I breathe out. If I'm going to get anywhere with this man, I need to smooth things over. He's never going to fall for my seduction if I continue to reveal my quills.

Okay. You're right. There are others, but I don't like how we left things. I want to make amends. My stom-

ach clenches. God, does it feel horrible being even remotely nice to this man.

His response isn't as fast this time, and my nerves tighten even more. *Did someone hack your email?*

No, this is Carmen Badson.

Hmm, that sounds like something a hacker would say. Is he being funny? Or does he honestly think my email has been hacked? I reread our messages. No, he's just being a dick. What's new?

Well, if I am a hacker, you can arrest me at the police station tomorrow when we meet. Weak response, but he's not giving me much to work with.

You really want to be put in handcuffs twice this week?

So am I a hacker or Carmen?

Regardless, I could predict the meeting will end up with one of us detained.

My heart races, and an intrusive thought pops into my mind. I type it, hit send, and throw my phone. I stare at the screen on the ground from my porch swing, my knees brought up to my chest, and my fingers clamped by my lips.

It takes a while—forever in fact, but the screen lights up again. I scramble off the bench and grab the phone. Reading the response to my email, which said, *Do you like that sort of thing?*

This is why we can't meet. Shit. Time to backpedal. What did I expect him to say? Humor and him are like water and oil.

Oh, God. I didn't mean it like that. I just meant, do you enjoy your job? Lie.

Sure. Is that why you want to meet? To ask me about my job satisfaction. That can be an emailed response.

No, that's not why I want to meet. I'm just trying to be friendly.

I'm starting to actually think you've been hacked.

I groan. He's so annoying, but I can't deny the tremble in my fingers as I type my response. *Why would someone hack me to get to you?*

Don't ask me to explain the logic of a criminal. Ironic, since he's more than likely behind the disappearance and murders of multiple women. I don't say this, obviously.

Listen, we can keep going back and forth, or you can agree to meet with me tomorrow afternoon at the station. All I want to do is apologize and explain the reason for my... I can barely type it, *unkind behavior.*

Idk, this is fun.

I smile unknowingly, shaking my head when I realize. *Okay, I'm going to take that as a "Yes, Carmen. I'll meet with you tomorrow at 4 p.m."???*

He takes a while to respond. I don't move, staring at my phone. *Fine, but no skirts.* I reread the message five times. What the fuck is he talking about? No skirts?

I just send back question marks.

Wear pants.

No fucking way is he telling me what to wear. Is that the problem? He hates me because I show up in my little skirts. What a fucking dick?

Why? Because I want to hear this.

I don't want you distracting anyone from their job.

Why does every cop in this town forget who I am? Does he know what I could do with this email? I want to tell him just that, curse at him, and never speak to him again, but obviously, I can't do that. Instead, I send, *Fine, I'll come at six p.m. so it's just you and me, and there's no one else to distract.* I hit send and turn on my away button. I might get a reply, but I want him to know that's the end of this conversation from me.

My plan will probably work better this way, considering I'm trying to seduce him. I must be careful, though. If I lay it on too thick, he'll suspect something. One thing is for certain, I'm wearing the fucking shortest skirt I own.

7

RAINING PIGS

I hate myself for wearing this stupid fucking skirt. It's short, skin-tight, and matches my black long-sleeve shirt, almost making it look like one piece. I am wearing stockings, even if they're sheer and do shit to protect me from the damp cold blowing in on the ominous grey clouds. I tuck my hands into my armpits. It's summer. It shouldn't be fifty fucking degrees, but I guess that's what I get for living in Dayton, Washington, and not somewhere warm and tropical. Here I go again, talking about leaving this place.

I walk up the sleek concrete steps to the police station, doing my best not to slip from the mist forming around me. I'm always punctual, and I look at my watch to see it's precisely six o'clock as I walk through the double glass doors. The office is empty, which is a bummer because I'd love to see Lucy at the front desk and catch up. Her chair isn't empty, though; the back of it faces me as I walk in. Upon the door closing behind me, its occupant swivels around to face me. Brick's grey-brown hair is neatly in place. He pulls off his circular glasses and puts them in the front pocket of his brown blazer. He's ungodly tall, muscular to a point it almost looks painful. I'm surprised the chair doesn't collapse under the sheer weight of him.

His eyes scan me intently, running from the top of my head to my boots. He sighs, shaking his head, already disappointed with me and I don't have to guess why. He stands, and his eyes dart. "Shall we?" He motions down the hall to his office. I nod, following after him. I'm surprised he didn't say anything about my skirt, even if his displeasure sat in the lines of his expression.

He opens his office door, taking a seat behind his large wooden desk. He folds his hands in front of him, and I don't miss the veins bulging as if he were straining. His eyes motion to the chair before him, but I pretend to miss it. Instead, I walk around his office, examining the shelves lining the walls. I stop at one filled with books. "Have you read all of these?" I ask.

"Yes," he replies plainly.

I bend over, reaching for a book on the lower shelf. I'm supposed to seduce him, after all.

He inhales. "Can you fucking sit down?"

I whip around, eyes wide. Yes, he's always been an asshole to me, but this is a little much. It catches me off guard, and I walk to the seat across from him, plopping down and studying him. His eyes look any-where but at mine. He appears different than he did moments ago, larger, as if his muscles are about to burst from him. Arm hair pokes out from his jacket sleeve and above his collar. It's almost like he's about to shift involuntarily. This just confirms his differ-entness. It wouldn't shock me if he were part-were-wolf and working for the Hunters. There have been rumors of part-Weres bred solely to take down the werewolf species. Seems counterintuitive to me. Why would they birth the very thing they're set on destroying? I guess it was never really about eradicating werewolves. It's about controlling us.

I don't say anything, an odd gesture for me, just cross my legs, wanting to make him squirm. It's working. He rubs at his arms as if he's itchy. "Sorry. I didn't mean to be rude."

It shocks me. I don't reply though, waiting for him to explain more. "It's just been a long day, and I'm anxious to get home."

"Oh, I'm sorry. I didn't mean to..."

He holds his hands out. "No, it's fine. It's fine. Just what did you want to talk about?"

Shit. I actually don't have much to say. My mission was to seduce him, but I'd been so insistent on meeting him here, and now it seems he's eager to get home. This isn't working in my favor. "I wanted to apologize for showing up at the crime scene and for my behavior."

He raises an eyebrow and looks me in the eye for the first time since I arrived. "That's not very like you."

Dick. I shove away my annoyance. I lean forward, resting my elbows on his desk. I mean it to be casual and sexy, but Brick pulls back as if being close to me repulses him. God, he must really fucking hate werewolves. Or maybe it's just me. "With everything going on with the missing women, I just have been stressed, and I realize that taking it out on you isn't the answer. We need to work together if we want to find the missing girls and bring justice to the ones that were slain."

"Right." He clears his throat. He doesn't question me about the missing girls. Grimm said the police washed their hands of the disappearances, claiming they ran away. I wonder if Brick is one of the officers who agrees with this notion. He doesn't deny that women are missing, as if he knows they are. If I weren't already suspicious of him, my alarms would be blaring right now.

"Is that it?" he asks, squeezing the life out of his hands again. Maybe I should be nervous around Brick. Clearly, he's about to jump out of his skin just from being near me. If he's working with the Hunters, he could be a threat to me, especially with his otherness. We're alone in his office with no one else in the building. He could kill me, but he'd be stupid to do that. It would be too messy.

"Um," I try to think of something else to say. I don't have a date lined up with him, and I seem to be doing a piss-poor job to get him to like me. I need more time.

He stands with a sigh. "Like I said over email, this could have been an email. You're wasting my time." He walks to the door as if to show me out. I can't take it anymore. I pop to my feet. "Why do you have to be such a dick?" I yell.

He laughs. "There we are. It was starting to freak me out with how unlike yourself you were being."

"I'm trying to be nice and turn a new leaf. Why do you have to make this so hard?"

He steps toward me. "Carmen, we do not get along. We are two different people. There's no need to turn a new leaf. We can just avoid each other."

My mind replays all our interactions in the past. Sure, I got on him about putting away the people who have killed Weres. I've been pushy and angry, but I still don't understand why he hates me so much. Obviously, he must hate werewolves if he's working with the Hunters, but I've seen how he interacts with the other Weres in our pack. He's never as hostile to them. "Well, guess what. You're not getting rid of me.

I don't understand why you hate me so much, but I will do whatever I can to make you like me."

"What? Why would you do that? Carmen, you don't like me either."

I step toward him, even as he backs away. This is not my usual approach. I never have to corner a man to get him to like me, but it's all I have left at this point. "Maybe I do like you, Brick. Maybe I want to spend more time with you." Our chests touch. He looks down at me, his eyes heavy and confused. I don't turn away from his gaze, getting lost in his smoky eyes. I've been this close to him before, but something feels different, familiar, and new at the same time. The moment stills, my heart beats quickly, waiting for what he'll say next. He moves in, a fraction of an inch closer, but then something washes over his face, and he moves around me. "I don't know if you have a personal vendetta to screw every single officer in the station, but I don't want to be a part of whatever game you're playing."

His words chill me to my core. I knew he always had an issue with me sleeping around with Straw and Wood. Has he been jealous all this time? Or does he just think I'm a slut and doesn't want to get tangled in my web? Suddenly, all of this seems so stupid. I don't need to seduce Brick. This was a horrible idea, and for what? To be verbally assaulted? I don't need him to save those girls. I'm done.

I walk toward the door, ready to slam it behind me, but the lights shut off, and a downpour of rain sounds around me.

8

FAKE PIGS

"Shit," I say, staring at the gray wall of water separated by the glass door of the police station. Brick sighs beside me, clicking off his phone and putting it in his pocket. "It looks like it'll be like this for the next few hours."

I don't say anything, just stare out at the expanse of grey, debating if I should take my chances, shift, and run home.

As if reading my mind, Brick says, "We should stay here until it passes. It'll be dangerous. I'll go find some candles." I don't know why he's pretending to give a crap about my safety. He obviously hates me and wants me and my kind dead. Minutes ago, this would have been the perfect situation for seduction, but now that plan is the furthest thing from my mind. What he said kind of hurt. I've always been proud of my sexuality, but the past few days have felt like the world is waging war on my womanhood, and Brick's words are like the nail in the coffin. I'm more than a piece of ass, I know that, but I'm getting a little tired of everyone viewing me that way.

I sigh, rolling back my shoulders and sitting on the visitors' couch in the corner. I pull out my phone. Great, it's dead. I can't even distract myself with mindless scrolling. Brick emerges from the hallway moments later, carrying two candles, clearly on their last legs, and a bag of chips. "Found these in the kitchen." He throws the bag to me before lighting the candles and placing them on the coffee table. He sits in one of the leather chairs across from me.

I open the bag of chips and begin eating, not offering a thank you or meeting his eyes. I can feel the nervous energy radiating off him. He squirms in his seat, shifting his legs from one over the other. He's probably not used to the absence of my rage. Good, I hope he feels like a dick.

"Carmen," he finally says, his voice heavy and low. He leans forward, his elbows on his knees, his arms outstretched. I divert my attention before I succumb to the guise of innocence he's attempting to display.

"Carmen, I'm sorry."

I don't respond. I don't forgive him.

"You came here to make amends, and I've been a dick."

"Correct."

"It's just with everything going on—the murders, it's a lot. And every time I see you, my failures stare me dead in the face."

I disarm myself, dropping the bag and looking at him completely. He's not confessing to me, at least, not directly. His statement could mean a million different things, but this is the perfect segue to discover more. "All I want is to help those girls, to help my clan. That's why I'm a reporter. That's why I bug the crap out of you every chance I get."

He smiles—a goddamn smile. I don't think I've ever witnessed one from him, and it makes me want to take a picture and keep it forever. It fades as fast as it comes, a sadness overtaking his features. A moment of silence passes us again. The only sound is the pounding against the roof. He breaks it. "I don't hate you, you know."

I cross my legs, leaning in close. "You literally told me you'd rather the council send anyone else besides me."

His eyes search me, stopping at my lips. "I have other reasons for saying that besides hating you." My mind replays his digs and comments over the years, paired with his recent outburst about sleeping with the police officers he supervises. Could he like me? Could all this be some weird way to mask his true feelings for me? Damn, I know I'm hot, but he sure sucks at letting me know how he feels about me. No, that can't be it. How could I miss it? Wouldn't it benefit him to get me on his good side? He's doing a piss poor job at it, but he's been so willing to apologize tonight. He's hated me all these years. Nothing has changed. What if he's playing the same game I'm playing—using me to get the council off his back, to find more locations of vulnerable women? Maybe it's as hard for him as it is for me.

The room darkens. The candles before me, doing an abysmal job previously at providing illumination, are now completely dim. "Shit," he mutters, inspecting the empty black glass. "I think I have more candles in my office somewhere." He connects his eyes with mine, tilting his head toward the hallway to signal me to follow.

A part of me, a large part, wants to refuse and stay right where I am. I'm not afraid of the dark, and being without Brick's presence sounds like a small dose of paradise within the uncomfortable situation I've volunteered myself. But then it's just that. I volunteered to find out more by using Brick. Sitting alone with him in his dark and information-riddled office sounds like the perfect situation for the cause. I get up and follow after him.

When I enter, he's already rummaging through his desk, muttering profanities with each abandoned drawer. "I think there might be some in the supply closet," he says, charging for his door. I have half a mind to tell him to calm the fuck down about the candles. I can easily shift to my night vision, but this is actually perfect. Now, I'm alone in his office.

I don't waste time walking to his desk and rummaging through the files on top. I would have thought my search would have taken longer, but lo and behold, the second file I pick up is the one. It's unnamed, but inside are pictures and police reports of all three missing girls.

"What are you doing?" Brick asks, a ridiculous amount of candles cradled in his large arms.

I drop the file, clearly guilty. "I was trying to see if you missed the candles in your desk."

He sighs, dropping the candles on a coffee table in front of a small sitting area in the corner of his office. "Inside a manila folder?" he asks in a dry tone.

"I got distracted?" My voice raises an octave.

He pulls the lighter out of his pocket and works on lighting each of the tiny, mismatched candles he managed to scrounge together, clearly unbothered by what I hold in my hand.

It unnerves me, and I stumble over my words. "Well, now that you've caught me, what is this?"

"It's a file on the missing girls," he says plainly. He sits back on the small couch in front of the coffee table, a macrame of candles sitting before him, so bright that it resembles a bonfire. He outstretches his arms over the back cushion, taking as much room as possible.

I step around his desk. "Why do you have a file on them? I thought you guys declared them runaways."

He nods, his stare so intense it makes my knees buckle. "Yes, that's what the other police officers have decided. You know I'm one of the only officers on the force who knows about the Weres, right?"

"So you're investigating this on your own?"

"No."

"Why?"

"I brought it up to the Department of Supernatural. They've taken it out of my hands."

Ah, the ominous "National Department of Supernatural." I always hear about them but never actually see their effects. It seems they're only mentioned so the police can do whatever they want and have a higher power to blame their shortcomings on. Brick is lying. I don't need powers to tell that. Even though he's staring at me head-on, his eyes dart subtly as if he's trying to prove something to me. Besides, if the Department of Supernatural truly took the case out of his hands, why would he have the file on the top of his desk?

I don't mind the lie. I expected it. If anything, it confirms that Brick knows something. He has an interest in these girls, and if I can stick close to him long enough, maybe I can find out where he's keeping them.

I move toward him, plopping down in the nonexistent space beside him on the couch. Part of my ass-cheek rests on his thigh, and I nuzzle in under his still-extended arm. I expect him to retreat, fold from his man-spread, and give me as much room as possible. Maybe even enjoy my closeness briefly before darting away, but he does neither. He looks down at me, his eyes zoned in my lips, a smirk at the corner of his lips.

The sight of him, the smell of him, the warmth of his presence so close, it catches me off guard. I never would have thought I'd have such a reaction to him. Of course, molten lava runs through my veins whenever I'm near him, but I always attribute that to my hate for him. Now, he's not yelling at me. He's not turning his nose away from me as if I disgust him. He's just watching me as if he wants to devour me. It's doing something to me, and I hate it even though I don't hate it.

My hands move on their own, leaving my personal space and traveling to his chest. My touch is light, but I recognize the hardness of his chest immediately. I lean in, the tiniest bit. Part of me wants to make him want me, but also, I need to know what he tastes like. Is it smokey like the rest of him? Is it sweet to make up for all of his sour? Or is it as rotten as his soul? I need to know.

He gets closer, but my eyes don't leave his, studying for any subtle movement that might give him away. All awareness moves to a point in my body. His hand inches to my thigh, pressing into my flesh. His touch sears me, melting me to the point until it's all I can think about. Men have touched every inch of me, especially my favorite places, but nothing compares to this simple touch. It makes everything more confusing. He's a man first and my enemy second. I can bring him to his knees. That's what this is. He wants me—carnally.

Our space closes, but before our skin touches, I catch his smile curve upward. It's subtle but noticeable. I pull back, and the smile grows. His eyes don't match, holding something vicious and knowing. Could he really be playing the same game I am?

There are so many layers to whatever this is between us, and I can't decipher where we are. I know my mission, though. At least I know that.

I grin sweetly, and he shakes his head with a smile as if reading all the thoughts bouncing around my head. It is as if we both know exactly what we're doing and are prepared to see this through. To confirm my thoughts, he clears his throat and creates some distance between us. Not an, *I hate you get away from me,* distance, but more of a, *let's not get carried away,* space. "I want to take you to dinner," he says, his gaze nowhere near mine.

"Dinner? Why?"

He laughs, shaking his head. "To make amends."

I show my hand. "Hm, big change of heart for someone who just moments ago didn't think amends were necessary." We're past this point in an unspoken way, but I want to know how he'll explain his sudden desire to be near me again.

"I think I needed the lights to go out to ground me. There's no way I'm leaving this place in the rain, so it made me sit here with you."

I fain empathy. "Oh, I'm so sorry. Sounds horrible."

He smiles again. God, it guts me. He turns to me, his elbows resting on his knees. "It actually wasn't horrible."

I squint an eye. "I gave you the silent treatment and went through your things."

"And surprisingly, I didn't hate it."

"So that's it, you like when I'm quiet and do my justice snooping without bugging you?"

He runs his fingers through his hair as if frustrated, but the small laugh shows otherwise. "Just let me buy you dinner to do some ounce of repayment for my horrible comments. We might not get along, but the way I spoke to you crossed a line. A bag of chips and an apology isn't going to cut it for me."

I stare at him with scrunched lips as if contemplating. I should agree, of course. This is exactly what I am here to gain—more access to his time. But I must put up somewhat of a fight to seem legit. After about five seconds, I consider my attempts a success. "Okay, I will have dinner with you, but..."

"But?"

"But you have to tell me one nice thing about me."

"What?"

"I know that will be hard for you, but I need to know you enjoy some part of my company. I don't want to force you to be near me if you hate everything about me."

"I don't hate everything about you."

"Then tell me what you like."

He studies me for a long moment, his stare heavy. I can't tell if it's hard for him to pick something, or there's just so many he doesn't know which one to choose. Who am I kidding? I know it's the former.

"I like your pinky."

"My pinky?"

"Yes."

"Why?"

He sighs, shaking his head, sitting back, and taking in the view of me. "Because it's a safe answer." His eyes drill into my pores.

"Safe," I say, accepting his meaning, even if I only have a guess as to what it is.

The lights crawl to life like electronic bugs flapping their wings. It's then I notice the rain outside has subsided. Our conversation seemed to cloud the environment around us, making coming to reality jarring.

I straighten, rising to my feet. "Well, it looks like we can both leave now. I bet you're relieved."

He stands as well, straightens his jacket, and gives me a confused look.

"You said you were eager to get home."

Recognizing dawns on his face. "Right, yes." I nod, walking toward the door. "Let me walk you out." He follows after me. We're silent until we reach the glass doors, leading out into the parking lot.

He seems nervous now. God, so much can change between two people in such a short amount of time. Before I reach the door handle, he clears his throat. "So, tomorrow night, for dinner?"

"Right. Um, yeah, sure. That works."

"Great." A hopeful smile washes over his face, and it's odd. How is he such a good actor? Maybe he wants to fuck me, but there's no way in hell he's suddenly decided he likes me. Nothing has truly changed between us. We're just both on the same page with pretending, and we're both fucking fantastic at it.

9

A PIG IN LIPSTICK

"Ouch!" I yell, holding my hand to my recently burnt scalp.

"Sorry!" Red pulls the crimper away from me and leans over to see her damage.

"Would ya' just stop trying to burn all my hair off?"

She tsks. "You're the one who wanted me to do your hair. You can't be needy and whiny." She moves to the next section of my dwindling locks.

"I asked you to do my hair, not ruin it."

"Ha, ha. Well, it actually looks pretty fucking good, so I would stop complaining." She turns me around to face the vanity mirror behind me. Staring back at me is an image of myself. Same dark brown hair, metallic brown eyes, dusting of freckles, and my nose ring, but everything is a little different. I push a lock of my styled hair behind my ear, turning my chin to examine the winged eyeliner and new shade of red lipstick Red applied to my lips. I always wear make-up, but it feels like a scene in a nineties rom-com. Seeing yourself under someone else's creative enhancement is new and exciting. I nod with a smile.

"See you like it," she says, hitting my shoulder.

"It helps when you have such a perfect canvas." I caress my cheeks and throw back my head.

"You're annoying." Red rolls her eyes and waddles to her bed, attempting to pull herself onto the King mattress but struggles with a huff.

I can't feign mock annoyance at her comment for long. She's too cute and helpless. I run to her aid, hiking up her leg so she can ungracefully roll onto the bed. We'd be quite a sight to see if anyone walked in on us. Me in my black lacy bra and underwear, pushing a large pregnant woman onto a bed. I laugh once she groans, rolling to her side and grabbing a pillow next to her to shove between her legs. "That was enough physical exertion for me for the day."

I tuck a strand of bright red hair behind her ear, examining the dark bags under her green eyes. "You know you didn't actually have to help me get ready. I just wanted to hang out with you before I'm stuck in a hell of my own creation for the next few hours."

She props her head with her hand, staring at me. "And you need advice." She reaches and taps her fingers like tiny claws. "Would you hand me those chips?"

I do as I'm asked, passing her the bag before sitting on the floor and rummaging through the bag of clothes I brought. "Advice? Why do I need your advice?"

"Rude," she says through a mouth full of crispy potato skins. "I happen to be very skilled at acquiring information from the enemy and even more proficient at the art of seduction. Evidence A." She rubs a hand over her large belly.

I laugh. "If I end up pregnant after this, something has gone horribly wrong. And besides, you got knocked up by my brother. I wouldn't be bragging about that."

The bag of half-eaten chips hits the side of my head. "Rude! Your brother's hot and has a huge di…"

I pop to my feet, a black cotton dress in my hands. "Okay! Stop right there!"

She throws her head back with a laugh. "I love freaking you out."

I force my hand into the bag, pulling out a clump of chips and shoving it into my mouth. "You're not getting this back," I say, crumbs dropping from my lips.

"No!" she yells.

I toss them to the floor with a smile and step into the stretchy fabric. Just when the straps hit my shoulders, the bedroom door swings open. "What's going on?"

I scream. "Cameron! I could have been naked!"

"Ew!" he says, charging the bed and climbing toward his wife. "Why aren't you naked?" he asks, looming over her. Red giggles underneath him and attempts to push him away.

"Get out!" I yell, turning away from the disgusting smooch-fest happening before me.

"Um, this is my bedroom. You can't tell me to get out," Cameron says, eyes still fixed on Red.

"This is our bedroom." Red slaps a hand to his chest from underneath him. "And I want her here."

"I heard you two discussing me in rather explicit detail. I think I should be allowed to listen."

I catch a glimpse of the two kissing through giddy smiles through the reflection of the vanity mirror as I sweep off the remains of potato chips from my lips. I'm gonna throw up. I focus my attention back to myself with a groan. Upon closer inspection, I hate my dress, and I hate my lipstick. I grab a tissue and rub the shade off before climbing back to the floor to continue my search through my mess of garments.

"What are you doing?" Red asks, laying on her side to face me, Cameron spooning her from behind.

"I look too slutty. It's too obvious."

"Well..." Cameron says, his pitch rising an octave.

"Shut up, fuckface."

Red slaps him. "You don't look slutty. You look hot. Why do you seem nervous?"

My cheeks heat, and my eyes dart to her. "I'm about to go on a date with Brick. A man who's hated me for years and is working with the Hunters. This could end very badly." My mind replays my last fake date, only a few days ago. That was the definition of disaster. This time, I'm not drinking. Brick may still be able to overpower me, but I'll put up a hell of a fight.

Cameron scoots to the head of the bed, leaning against the headboard. "Grimm told you what to plant?" he asks, his voice all serious now.

I sigh, pulling out a short forest green dress. It's basically the same style as the one before, but something about green seems less sultry than black. At least, I think. "Yes, I will mention how Josie is supposed to be home alone tonight, and I'm worried about her. If the Hunters show up at Josie's house, we know Brick is our man."

"I don't understand," Red asks. "Don't we already know that Brick is our man? How does this help us?"

"I mean, we're pretty sure," I counter, walking toward their closet, shutting the door behind me, and raising my voice so they hear me through the slats. "His aloof behavior to the disappearances, him talking to Richard, and the file on his desk, are all damning pieces of evidence, but we need to be sure."

"Then what?" Red asks.

I step out of the black dress. "Then I make him fall in love with me and find out where those girls are."

A knock comes from the other side of the house. "Are you expecting anyone?" Cameron says, his voice coated with alarm.

"Brick's picking me up here," I shout, glancing at my watch. "But he's not supposed to be here for another thirty minutes." I knew I wouldn't have enough time to get ready and return home. I sent an email this morning to tell him to pick me up at my brother's. He responded just as quickly as he did two days before and confirmed the time. I really needed to get his number. Conversing through email feels like I'm dating a personification of corporate America.

"I'll check." I listen as Cameron jumps to the floor and walks toward the front door. Seconds later, he yells, "It's him."

I pop my head out of the closet. "What a dick! Who shows up early? I'm not ready."

Red struggles to sit up as I exit the closet, pulling the green dress overhead. "We know he's a dick. Brick the dick. Ha. That's funny. Besides, you look great. You're fine."

Cameron enters the room again when the dress is halfway down my ass. "Get out!" I yell. "Stall him."

He turns his back to me but remains in the doorway. "I want to hear what you both are talking about. I feel left out. Besides, I don't want to hang out with Brick. I'm not good at faking things."

I straighten my dress, examining myself in the mirror. "Don't you want to go stare him down? Act all alpha male protecting your little sister."

"No."

"Why? You seemed to love doing that with Kilo."

"Oh, I want to hear what happened with Kilo," Red says with a giddy cadence.

"That's different..."

Brick knocks again, louder this time.

Red sighs. "Oh, Cameron, go get the door."

"Fine." He shuts the bedroom door behind him.

I lean over, dabbing on a sheer lip gloss before straightening my dress and tucking and untucking my hair behind my ears.

"Why do you seem so nervous?" Red whispers. The males' low voices seep through the doorway's cracks.

I shoot her a dumbfounded look from the mirror's reflection before turning to her. "I'm about to go on a date with a potential Hunter and plant fake information to incriminate him. Besides, he's some sort of powerful creature that none of us know about. Of course, I'm going to be nervous."

Red shrugs. "So. Defeating Hunters is the kind of stuff you live for. You've been waiting for your chance to bring them down at the paper, and now the council is giving you a chance to actually kick some ass." She squints an eye at me. "Do you *like* him?"

"No!" I whisper-scream much too quickly. "I definitely don't like him."

"Carmen! Are you ready?" Cameron yells, clearly uncomfortable.

I turn, giving myself another examination before walking toward the door and slipping on my black strappy heels. "Good luck!" Red calls before pulling her comforter over her head. I enter the living room to find Brick seated on an armchair by the front door, Cameron pouring a scotch into a chilled highball glass.

His eyes catch mine, his pupils dilating, but then he turns his head and takes a big gulp of his drink. He's wearing a white button-down, the top two buttons undone, revealing a peek of his tanned and broad chest. He spreads his legs wide, his tight gray pants barely leaving anything to the imagination. Damn, he looks good. He usually looks like such a fucking dork, but his hair is even styled differently, less in place, and pushed back.

My eyes wander longer than they should. I shake my head, riding the distracting thoughts from my mind. Why would he dress differently for our date? Is he doing what I'm doing? Trying to impress me to get more information out of me? It's the only thing that makes sense. I steel my expression, a slight shake of my chin. "You're early." I should try to be charming, but it's just not me. He'll catch on if I don't give him shit, especially if it's something that's so clearly annoying.

He shrugs, a mischievous sparkle in his eye. "It's better than being late."

"Not really." I cross my arms.

Cameron picks up a glass on the coffee table, walking toward me with the crystal decanter. "Here, why don't you take a drink before you go?" He widens his eyes and clenches his lips. Clearly, a signal to stop acting like a bitch, or I'm going to blow the mission.

I take a shallow breath. "No, thank you," I say through a forced smile.

"You sure?" Cameron tries again, pushing the glasses closer to me.

"I'm fine." My smile fades.

Brick clears his throat and stands. "Okay, well, we should get going."

I want to say that we have all the time in the world since he so rudely decided to show up early. Thankfully, for his sake, I'm always ready a bit early. I'd like to have more time with Red and Cameron to discuss the plan for this dinner or even just some time to decompress, but nope. Brick is set on making my life difficult. Instead of lying and saying I'm almost ready and hiding out with Red for some time, I nod, plastering on a small smile. "Yep, let's get going." Besides, I don't want Cameron to reveal everything before the plan starts. He's a mess with the baby on the horizon. One second, he's about to kill everyone in sight; the next, he's cuddling Red like a lost puppy. He's not on his A-game, and having Brick around him for any more time is a risk.

I step closer to Brick, taking in his strong, musky scent. It's unlike anything I've ever smelt before—his own personal fragrance. If I had to name something similar, I'd say smoke, but that could just be because everything about him reminds me of smoke—harsh, illusive, something for secrets to hide in. I stare up at him, still impossibly tall even in my heels, and I'm not very short. He stares down at me. His gaze intense and hard to read. He doesn't scan me over like I did when I first caught his new look. Instead, his eyes tether to mine as if looking away would be too dangerous. But then his eyes drift to the top of my head. He reaches out, and my breath stops. He grabs a strand of my hair between two fingers. "Did you burn your hair?" he asks, a smile inching up the corner of his lips.

I'm knocked out of whatever the hell he just pulled me into. I take a step back, my hard exterior dropping back in place. "Red did it." Is all I muster, biting my lip from saying more. No compliments on my appearance or kind gesture, just scrutiny. How very Brick of him. I'm still convinced he's attempting to draw me in as much as I am to him, but he's not trying very hard. Or maybe he's just doing what I'm doing—not wanting to lay it on too thick to seem unbelievable. Only one of us can win at this game, and there's no universe where a wolf doesn't outsmart a pig.

10

PIG DINNER

There is only one semi-fancy restaurant in town, so I don't even ask Brick where we're heading. We drive through the quiet streets of Dayton in his gray, old-fashioned Buick. If he weren't so good-looking, it would look like a car for a serial killer. Except he very well may be a murderer, so it actually fits him in a whole Ted Bundy type of way. I attempt to start a conversation, pointing to an old building as we pass. "It looks like they're renovating the McClary House. I hope they don't strip it of all its character."

He shrugs. "Yeah, we'll see."

I study his clean-shaven side profile. The pores on his chin are already dark with his smoky hair, wanting to peek through. He grips the steering wheel, his knuckles white. Am I annoying him already? What's the point of this dinner if he doesn't want to talk to me? This is going to be a long date. Maybe if I'm lucky, it'll be so dull for him too, that he'll rush right through it and take me home full and unscathed. But even as the hopeful thought passes my consciousness, I know that can't be my goal. He won't fall in love with me if I'm boring. I need to stroke his ego, at least. Besides, he's trying to get something from me as much as I'm trying to get something from him. It should be fairly easy to get him to keep me around.

I abandon my attempts to create small talk on the way to the restaurant. Maybe he gets car sick. Hell, if I know. Just when the silence is about to wither away my last ounce of reserve, Brick pulls into an empty parking spot at, low and behold, Gwendolyn's, the town's only nice Italian restaurant. Thankfully, the place has a kick-ass chicken parm and a superb wine list, but unfortunately, I'm not drinking tonight. I have to do this date stone-cold sober, and I already could use a drink.

I fidget while stuffing my phone into my small purse and unbuckling my seat belt. I startle when my door opens. I turn to Brick holding the door for me, looking straight ahead instead of my quizzical stare. "Thank you," I say as I exit the car. He grunts with a nod and leads me into the restaurant.

It's a Tuesday night, so the place is pretty bare. We're seated at a white linen table in the middle of the low-lit restaurant and given a small drink menu each. I pretend to examine the contents. Before the hostess even leaves, Brick clears his throat. "Get me a scotch on the rocks." The young woman, who's not our server, nods, a slight panic in her eyes. I have half a mind to yell at him and tell him to cool his jets. I used to be a server, and it's not easy when guests try to order things from the hosts, but I let it slide. He's desperate for a drink, and I won't get in his way.

The real waitress comes back shortly, scotch in tow, and takes my drink order of a Diet Coke. Before she leaves, Brick takes a big sip of his beverage and orders another one. Jesus Christ, I hope he's coherent enough to register the fake information I plant.

I fold my hands before me when we're alone again, trying to gain Brick's attention. He's fidgety, scratching at his long sleeves. "Brick," I call.

He smiles and finally looks me in the eyes. "You know my name isn't Brick, right?"

"Your name isn't Brick?" Great, I'm on a date with a man whose name I don't even know.

He smiles and finishes his first drink with a big gulp. He doesn't even flinch as the alcohol runs down his throat. "Well, it's my last name."

Yeah, that makes sense. I laugh. It seems to shock him, and his eyes grow wide as he takes me in, his gaze flicking from my lips to my eyes. "Okay, what's your name?" I ask.

"It's Bryce."

"Bryce." I roll the word around on my tongue. It suits him, I guess. "Can I keep calling you Brick?"

"Call me whatever you want." His eyes sear into mine. The waitress places his next drink beside him, and he takes a sip without breaking eye contact. His disposition changes by the second. One minute, he seems about to jump out of his skin, the next, he holds me with a stare only fit for a man in control. He almost reminds me of a Were on the brink of a Blood Moon.

The more I get to know him, the more I doubt we share paranormal ancestry. He's different, even more different than my furry flavor.

"Do you guys know what you'd like yet?" the waitress asks in a high-energy voice.

I hadn't even looked over the menu, but I don't want to make this dinner any longer than it needs to be. "Do you have a special?" I ask.

"Yes, tonight's special is a balsamic glazed porchetta."

"That's pork, right?" Brick asks, his tone all business.

"Yes."

"No, we're not getting that." He looks back down at his menu.

I grab the waitress' attention, silently pleading for forgiveness for my counterpart's rudeness. I guess he's deciding what I can and cannot eat. Maybe he's Jewish and doesn't eat pork. Fuck if I know. "I'll have the chicken parmesan, please." I study Brick, wondering if he will refuse that as well.

He passes his menu to the waitress. "I'll have the same." He gives a polite nod and takes another sip of his drink. "And another one of these." Jesus fucking

Christ. This guy is either an alcoholic or about to be hammered.

The waitress tells us our food will be right out, and then it's just Brick and I alone again. The alcohol must be calming his nerves because now, instead of scanning his eyes around the restaurant, he glues them to me. It's completely unfair since I'm stone-cold sober and feel every inch of his gaze. While I have his attention, though, I might as well make the best of it. I push out my tits and lean slightly over the table, lazily dragging my finger in a circle on the white tablecloth. "Sorry if I seem tense tonight," I say, staring at my hands and fluttering my eyelashes.

"Oh." It's quick, but his eyes dart to my cleavage and then back to my eyes. *Yes, my charms are working.*

I sigh, "Yeah, it's just this girl that I used to babysit when I was in high school, Josie. She will be home alone tonight and refuses to let anyone stay with her." He doesn't say anything, so I go on. "I'm so worried that she's going to be the next girl kidnapped or worse." This part isn't that hard to act. I am truly worried for all these girls, even if Josie isn't home alone tonight or anywhere near her secluded home in the woods.

Brick brings his drink up to his lips. "Can't you send some people to watch her house?" It's a good question, potentially a plot hole in my made-up story. My brain scrambles for a lie.

"Everyone's busy scouting the other young women's houses. Josie was adamant that she doesn't want anyone babysitting her and for the pack to use their resources on someone else." Whether it's the alcohol or my tits, the lie doesn't send off Brick's alarms. He stares at me, leaning forward, a hungry look in his eyes as he traces the rim of his near-empty glass.

I smile and tuck a strand behind my ear. This is the exact reaction I wanted out of him, but I can't deny the moment's intensity. It takes me off guard, and I have no choice but to flush. My nerves seem to knock Brick out of his trance. He mutters *fuck* under his breath, so subtly, but I'm watching him too closely to miss it. He downs the rest of his drink right as the waitress brings him his next one and takes a sip from the fresh glass. He looks to the side, annoyance written across his face.

"Wow, what is that, your fourth?" I ask, unable to hide the twinge of annoyance in my voice.

He furrows his brow, examining his drink. "I'm not sure. I don't normally drink."

"You don't normally drink?"

"No," he says in an annoyed tone. Either he's a mythical being who can't get drunk, or he will be obliterated any second now. God, he must fucking hate me if he must turn into an alcoholic to be in my presence. I want to punch him in his stupid stone-cold face, but instead, I pop to my feet. "I need to use the restroom." I turn away from the table. I planned to drop the fake information and then give him some time alone so he could text the Hunters about Josie. This is as good a time as any. I don't know if he'll be too drunk to do it or if he even believed my half-ass story. I'd never forgive myself if this stupid date was all for nothing.

When I return to the table, my fury is contained after a few soothing breaths in the mirror. The food has arrived, and Brick is already going to town on his chicken parmesan. Red sauce is smeared over his face, and he barely looks up at me as he shovels the food into his mouth.

"I love coming back to the bathroom to find my meal," I say, unfolding a napkin and placing it over my lap.

He darts his eyes to mine for a second, nodding before taking a big chug of his fresh drink. This waitress seriously needs to cut him off. "This is really fucking good," he says, his words slur with a mouth full of food. *Oh no.* Here goes his decline. I'm not in the mood to take care of a completely inebriated, enormous man. I've had my fill of idiots for a lifetime. I'm starting to doubt he fell for my trap and texted the Hunters. Oh well, new plan. Convince his drunk-ass to give me information.

I take a bite of my food, watching him carefully. A smile lines his face between every bite, and his eyes shine. I've never seen him so happy. Who knew that a chicken parmesan could make him a more pleasant person? Or more likely, the swift shift has more to do with the excessive amount of alcohol running through his system. "I'm serious! This is so fucking good." He leans in as if to tell me a secret. "What do you think they put in this stuff? Is yours as good as mine? Let me try a bite." Before I can stop him, he snags a piece of my chicken with his fork, bringing it to his mouth.

His eyes grow wide as he chews. "Okay, no. Yours is so much fucking better." He stills for a moment, his smile fading. "Holy shit, are you beautiful."

I gasp with a laugh, taken off guard by his words. "Okay, buddy. I think that's enough scotch for you." I reach over and pull the cup away from him.

He grabs my wrist. "No, seriously. Have you seen yourself?"

I give a clenched-lip smile. "Thank you, Bryce. Is this your way of repaying me for the comment in the office?"

He grabs his face with both hands. "God, I'm an idiot. Why would I ever be mean to you?" He leans over; his head now rests on the tablecloth. "I know why I'm a dick to you, but I don't want to be. You're just so pretty. It's your smell. God, your smell, it makes me so angry."

"Okay," I say. So much for liking drunk Brick for a minuscule of a second. I catch the waitress with my eyes, motioning to the food as a silent plea to get us boxes so we can get the hell out of here.

She must have experience with drunk men because she scoops our food up, drops the bill, swipes my card, and gets us out of the restaurant in a matter of minutes. Brick is declining, and I have to hold him up as we walk to his car. He's fucking heavy. I can lift a car over my head, barely breaking a sweat, but something about this man dulls my powers. That, or whatever he is so much more powerful than I am, and that's something I don't want to consider.

I'm able to shove his huge body into his passenger side and buckle him in. He starts giggling again as I drive down the road. I keep glancing at him, amazed at how his usual dominating presence can morph into such a docile drunk. Thank God, because if he turned violent, I could be in serious trouble.

"Shit," I mutter to myself once I realize I have no idea where Brick lives. I shake his arm. He jolts, banging his head against the window. "Huh?" He sits up straight.

"Where do you live?"

He laughs. "At my house, duh."

"Okay, I don't know where that is."

"Why? I know everything about you?"

"You know everything about me?"

He giggles. "Of course. I know you bought your two-bedroom house four years ago for two hundred fifteen thousand dollars." So, the man knows how to look up housing records. Weird, but he could have just been researching me before our date.

"Okay, well, I'm not a creep, so I did not look you up." Honestly, it's surprising I never did, but I've been too busy researching other Hunters over the years.

He turns to me, frowning. "It's probably because you hate me."

I sigh. "I don't hate you."

He leans against the window again. "Yes, you do. You've said as much."

"Okay, maybe I used to hate you, but we're turning a new leaf, remember? We're on a date."

"A date?"

"Yeah, remember you asked me on a date and then proceeded to get drunk as fuck, and now I'm having to take you home?"

He laughs. "Oh, yeah. Sorry."

"Whatever." Even if he wanted to tell me where he lived, I don't think he could gather his working brain cells together to do so. I drive in the direction of my house. He can sleep on the couch until he sobers up.

"It's just every time I'm around you, I can't control myself. And now I'm reminded of those girls."

"Those girls?"

"We need those girls. It's the only way."

"Brick." I shake his arm. His head bumps against the window. "What are you talking about?" But it's no use. He's out. "Fuck." It's not a confession, but damn is it incriminating.

I pull onto my small driveaway. He'll have to get up enough to get inside. There's no way I can carry him in when he's completely unconscious. I can only hope that he reveals more about the girls when he's jostled around.

I open the passenger door, and he falls like dead weight. I catch him just in the nick of time and thankfully, he comes to a bit, holding himself upright. "Woah, sorry about that," he says, his hands braced on my arms. Even in his stupid drunk state, his eyes take me in as if I'm a meal to be savored. I get lost in his stare momentarily, but it's broken as his body becomes heavier, and he falls into me. "Alright, buddy. Let's get you inside."

He stands with a wobble, using me for support. "Oh, we're at your house," he says excitedly, looking around as I walk him toward the front door. The porch steps are a bitch, but miraculously we make it through the door. I'm about to steer him to my couch, but one look at my measly purple piece of furniture, and I know he won't fit. He'll roll off in a matter of minutes, and although I'm inclined not to give a shit, the stupid good-hearted part of me insists he sleeps in my bed.

His consciousness blinks out the further we get into my house. Thankfully, it's small, so it only takes a few incredibly strenuous steps until we're in my bedroom, and I throw him into my bed. The second he hits my comforter, he's out, his breath heavy as if in a deep sleep.

I stare at him, catching my breath. If he had given me his address, I could have snooped through all his shit while he slept. The only thing I've accomplished from this date is a cryptic confession. I feel around his pockets. His phone is in the front one, not under his weight, and I didn't have to feel up his ass to find it. I don't know if I'm disappointed or relieved. I click it on but frown once I realize I don't know his password. He doesn't even have a fingerprint or facial identification. Annoying. I shove his phone back into his pocket, finally catching my breath.

My mind replays his mannerisms, comments, and gestures throughout the night, each one more confusing than the last. It's obvious he has an attraction to me. He called me beautiful, after all. It wouldn't be the first time a Hunter lusted after a werewolf. Just because you hate someone doesn't mean you don't want to fuck them. I can work with this.

I lie next to him, examining his unconscious form as I work through my thoughts. When he wakes up, it will be hard for him to continue his aloof act. Knowing him, he'll try, but if he asked me on a date to apologize for the rude comment at the station, after tonight's train-wreck, he'll have to propose. Okay, no, gross, but he's got some making up to do.

This date feels like a complete disaster, but this is technically good. Maybe he couldn't text the bait, but I dug my claws deeper into his heart. This wasn't supposed to take one night. Making him fall for me, a woman he hates, obviously wouldn't be easy. I'm on the right track, though. I feel it.

I watch his chest rise and fall, his lips slightly parted as his eyes twitch behind his eyelids. He's devastating when he's not being an ass. If only I could keep him just like this. I'll probably have to sleep with him to get him vulnerable enough to spill the Hunters' plans. I mull over the idea. Honestly, I don't think I'll hate it. He's big and beautiful, and a hate fuck sounds cathartic. But even as I ponder the notion, something twists inside me, an unknown feeling I don't want to untangle. My thoughts don't worry me too much because before I know it, my eyes grow heavy, and my consciousness blinks out.

11

PIGS IN A BLANKET

I t's delectably warm and cozy in my bed. My eyes won't open, but honestly, I don't even make a valor attempt. I'm too comfortable and snuggle in deeper. An arm wraps around my middle and pulls me close. Normal Carmen would freak the fuck out that someone is in my bed, their hand slowly making its way up my abdomen. But my brain quietly reminds my nerves that I fell asleep beside an incapacitated Brick. The comfort and sleep still gnawing on half of my consciousness make everything lighter and harder to resist.

His big hands emit the perfect temperature, and I lean into his touch, softly nudging him up my body. He doesn't heed my non-verbal requests at first, but when I place my hand over his and direct him to my breast, he doesn't resist. His touches are light, not breaking me from my trance but turning my insides into a warm liquid. He dives his hand underneath the neckline of my dress, teasing over the lace of my bra.

I press against him, my backside colliding with a wall of muscle. I arch my back, rubbing my ass against his hardened length. A heavy breath escapes me. He's impressively long, and I could spend the rest of the morning moving up and down his morning wood, even with our clothing separating us. That's not true, though. My body sings with anticipation, wanting him to relieve the inferno between my legs with his glorious rod.

His breath on my neck is heavy and strained. We're both moving so slowly, stealing brushes without breaking the fog settled over us. His fingers find their way under my bra, and I lean into his feather-light touch. It's teasing and sweet, and I could come undone just from the simple movement. A meek moan breaks through my lips, but I don't let more pass. A part of me knows that the only reason we're allowing this intimacy is because of the sleepy drunkenness settled over us. One wrong move and the shades open, waking us to reality. I want to enjoy this. In fact, I *need* release more than I need air.

His lips graze across the skin on the back of my neck. It's not a kiss, but I feel the wetness of his saliva and the stubble of his chin. I want his mouth all over me. I press closer into him, and he bucks his hips ever so slightly, grinding against my ass. I need more, so much more, but the gentleness is such a delicious torture that I'm happy to wade in the sticky waters of our lust.

His gentle swipes at my nipple cease, trailing down my abdomen. I can't stop my low moans. Brick groans from behind me, halting his thrusts and digging his nose into my shoulder. His hand grips at my side, squeezing me to steady himself. I remain completely still. We're so close to ruining this thing—this delectable, delirious pocket of time we've found ourselves.

Time starts up again, and Brick's breath evens. He continues crawling his hand down my side, pausing once he meets the hem of my dress halfway up my ass. The moment moves like melted chocolate as he works his way under the lace of my panties, pausing to restrain himself with every inch he gains. His rough fingers dance at my lips, dipping into my wetness. I press into him, and he allows his finger to slide through me. The small movement steals the breath from my lungs, and I grind myself against his touch.

His breath heats the space between my neck and my shoulder as he increases his tempo, both grinding against me and running his finger through the silky valley leading to my core. I'm so goddamn wet, making his moves even more erotic. His fingers tease at my entrance. I can't take it anymore. I need him inside of me.

"Brick," I whisper. I don't mean the words to leave my lips, but I'm too lost to think about anything but him. The moment my ears pick up the break in silence, I tense, waiting to see if I just ruined our silent contract. His scruff rubs up my neck, and his teeth graze my lobe. "You're so fucking wet for me, Carmen."

My moan mixes with my sigh of relief. I work my hips harder against him, rubbing against his shaft in a desperate motion. One of his fingers enters me, just a taste of what it would feel like wrapping around him. "Oh, God!" I cry, not afraid of words anymore.

"Jesus Christ, Carmen, you're so tight. I'd rip you in half." He's not lying. Just from the impression on my backside, I know he'd stretch me in all the right ways. He inserts another finger, fucking me harder as if to get me ready for what I hope is to come.

I reach behind me to grab him, but his other hand snakes underneath me and holds my hand against me. "No, I'm too close," he says through gritted teeth. Jesus Christ, he's about to come just from rubbing against me. My dress is up to my stomach, but he's still wearing his slacks from the night before. God, I want to feel his hottest point on me—in me, stretching me to my breaking point.

He inserts another finger while applying pressure to my clit with his thumb. "So good," I murmur, biting my lip as if the words are involuntary. He increases his pressure and speed at my words. I bet he'd be so responsive, so eager to please. Wet sounds fill my eardrums as he thrusts his fingers in and out of me. I'm so close to the breaking point I barely notice the shift happening behind me. It's slight but obvious. He's growing larger, all of him. His skin toughens, and as he presses his top teeth against my clavicle, I swear I feel the impressions of fangs. If I were in my right mind, I'd turn to catch his transformation, but I'm too lost, his dick rubbing against me, his fingers deep within me. Nothing could bring me out of this moment, not even an obvious monster grinding behind me.

The fear, mixed with intrigue, brings me to my breakpoint. I cry out, "Brick!" Ultraviolet colors cloud behind my eyelids. My body melts to Brick's whim. I'm not human anymore, just a vessel of liquid pleasure. Brick doesn't let up as my orgasm washes over me, still grinding against me. He whimpers. "Carmen, God," he says before he moans, loud and low in my eardrum. "Fuck." He falls to his back.

My head clears as he creates space between us. His arm is still trapped under my body, and he doesn't yank himself free. My eyes blink open, the reprieve lasting only a moment. Brick catches his breath, but I don't move yet, too mortified for what happens next. Brick just made me come. The man I loathe, the man who may have murdered members of my pack and betrayed us, just fucked me with his fingers until I cried his name and convulsed into a pile of mush. Not only that, but I just made him ejaculate, and he didn't even fuck me. He came from grinding against me and bringing me to pleasure. It's a powerful feeling, and maybe I would revel in it more if, just seconds ago, I wasn't in the mental state to drop to my knees and let him have me in any way he pleased.

My memory kicks in, reminding me of the shift I felt happening against me. I turn to Brick. His eyes clench shut, and his chest falls and rises as if he just ran a marathon. There's a subtle difference to him. His muscles seem larger, especially in his neck, almost as if he just pumped hundreds of pounds of iron, but whatever he turned into when he was holding back has gone.

His eyes shoot open as if dread dropped through his stomach. He sits up, ramrod straight. "Shit. I..." He doesn't look at me, but I can see his eyes darting and his panic morphing across his features.

I grab his arm. "Brick, it's fine."

He pulls his arm back, not aggressively, but enough to hurt my feelings. "I should go." He stands, walking toward my bedroom door. Before he completely disappears, he sticks his head back in with a sigh, finally looking me in the eye. "Sorry about... everything. I'll make it up to you."

"It's fine," I say, still lying down but turned to face him with my head propped up in my hand.

He nods, his eyes saying so much more than his mouth will allow. He walks out of view as my brain plays catch up. "Wait, how are you going to get home?" I ask, sitting up.

"I'll walk," he replies, the door shutting behind him.

I laugh. The man is going to walk to his house with cum lining the inside of his underwear. What a fucking sight to see.

12

LYING WITH PIGS

I'd hoped Grimm would give me until noon before blowing up my phone. Okay, he called once, but the volume was on max, and I was still enjoying the nap I'd fallen into after Brick left. I had decided I wasn't going into the office today. I planned to spend the day sleeping instead of dealing with the events that transpired the night before to this morning. Obviously, it was a stupid, optimistic thought. Grimm would want to know what happened. Those girls were still missing.

I pick up after the fifth ring, clearing my throat and tucking my hair behind my ear before speaking. "Hello."

"Are you alone?" Grimm asks, all business.

"Yes," I reply.

"Good. Kilo's on the line. They took the bait."

"What?"

"The Hunters fell for the information you planted. Jessica's house was infiltrated, and we had a small team capture two Hunters." Grimm's voice echoes through my skull. I replay the events from last night. How did Brick possibly gather the where-with-all to text the Hunters when I was in the bathroom? Was he even really drunk? I suppose his downfall didn't officially start until I came back from the restroom, but it all seems too implausible.

My mind races with images of just hours ago, his hands caressing my most sensitive flesh, his cock rubbing against my backside; it sours my gut. How could I let such a creature bring me so much pleasure? Now that it's confirmed that Brick is a double agent, my relationship with him only needs to thicken. I have to get him to fall in love with me—to pull him into my web until he's so intoxicated that he lets his guard down. It shouldn't be difficult, judging from the cum coating his briefs, but shame boils deep in my veins. Just because I need to get him obsessed with me doesn't mean I must enjoy the heat of him, and boy, did I enjoy myself—more than I want to admit.

The silence on the line falls to my attention, and a hopeful thought pops into my mind. "Did they interrogate the Hunters?"

Grimm sighs. "Yes, Red has been working with them to bring out any information...."

I cut him off. "Red? But she's..."

"Yes, she shouldn't be using her powers in her state or even be out of bed, but Cameron has been by her side, and she insists on helping in any way possible. You know how she is."

"Ugh, yes." I cringe at the thought of my best friend using her mind control powers so late in her pregnancy. She came into her powers only two years ago when the mating bond snapped into place between my brother and her. In fact, she didn't know she was part Were until she met him, and he revealed her family's history. Even though she's very new to her strength, she controls it like a badass superhero. It only works when the person she's using it on is in her presence, and it's difficult to wield. She could get the Hunters to admit what they knew but couldn't get them to return to their group and burn it all to the ground. Using her powers shouldn't hurt the baby, but she's supposed to be resting, not interrogating evil villains. I need to do more.

"Did she discover anything?"

"No, the two they sent seem to be new recruits. They don't know where they're hiding the other women, and the only names they mentioned were prominent Hunters."

"Brick?" My heart picks up a speed.

"They didn't mention Brick, no."

Kilo's voice breaks through. I'd almost forgotten he was on the line. "But obviously, we know Brick is working for the Hunters. How else would they have known?"

"Right," I reply, tightening my fists at my side.

"Carmen, how did the date go yesterday? Do you think you could continue?" Grimm asks.

I'm so thankful that this conversation is over the phone and not in person. My cheeks beat hot under the question, replaying the scene from this morning. "Yeah." My voice cracks, and I clear my throat. "I can try to get more information from him."

Kilo speaks. "Grimm and I were talking about offering you training. I was a special operations officer in the military, so I have experience in information extraction. I could give you some pointers."

He's offering to help me. It's nice because he's a nice guy, but I can't help the sense of annoyance running through me. Why am I the one spying on Brick when Kilo is apparently a bonafide spy? The rational part of my brain takes over. Obviously, Kilo can't distract Brick with tits, and I've got a fucking fantastic pair ready to use as weapons. "Yeah, that would be good," I reply.

"Great," says Kilo. "Are you free in about an hour? I could come over."

I look around the mess of my room. I changed into a grey lounge set once Brick left but haven't showered or brushed my teeth this morning, just falling right back into my nest of a bed where I'm currently perched. I jump to my feet with my cell phone still in hand. "Uh, yes. That could work."

"Great. I'll be there soon."

"Thank you again, Carmen. You are an invaluable member of our pack." Grimm's words swell a knot inside of me. It's nice to be appreciated, but also, he has no clue that I didn't do a lot of spying yesterday. Instead of pressing Brick for answers in his drunken state, I just allowed us to fall asleep together, wrapped in each other's arms, and in the morning, allowed him to strum me like a violin while I orgasmed to another realm. Maybe I do need Kilo's help because I've barely started my mission, and I'm already on a downward spiral.

***

Kilo is punctual as ever, and I throw the last dirty sock into my hamper right as his sharp knock sounds on my wooden front door. I straighten my plain white t-shirt before charging to the door, taking a deep breath as I pull it open.

"Hello," he says, his smile bright and his blue eyes as crisp as the sky behind him.

"Hi. Come on in," I respond, stepping out of the way so he can walk inside.

He does that thing all guys do when they step into a new place, look at the rafters as if gauging the structural integrity of the space. "You've got a nice home."

"Thanks." I motion to the armchair just steps away. "Have a seat. Can I get you anything to drink?" I ask, walking toward the kitchen, separated from the living room by a half-wall with an opening to see in and out.

"Sure. I'll take a water," he responds as he sits, outstretching his large legs.

I return seconds later with two chilled glasses of water and hand one to him before sitting on the couch across from him. I take a sip, attempting to kill time before I talk. I'm nervous, which isn't typical for me. Something about having a man in my home that I'm attracted to just hours after the other that made me come just left is an odd feeling. Maybe I feel a little guilty. Kilo saved me from Wood after he called me a slut. I don't want to confirm his words, even if everything I do is to help the pack. I try to convince myself of this even as I doubt its truth.

Kilo sniffs the air, and my blood solidifies. Weres have a keen sense of smell. Could he possibly smell Brick? "Do you use lemon Pine Sol?" he asks.

I sigh in relief, a bit more dramatically than I'd like. "Yes, I just mopped."

He chuckles. "That's what I use too."

"Cool."

God, this is painful. He may be hot, but our chemistry is a trickling stream. Is it because I'm still thinking about Brick flicking my nipples? No, it can't be. I cross my legs. "Where should we start?" I should ask him about his military training and learn more about his past, but I want to get this over with.

Kilo stands and sits next to me on the couch, turning to me. "Okay, so I completely trust your abilities, but just for a baseline, I need to see you tell a lie."

"Tell a lie?"

He scoots closer. "I want to see if you have any tells."

I laugh. "Well, I hope not. I've already been lying to Brick."

"I know, and so far, so good, but you'll have to start snooping through his stuff when he leaves, sending him away to give you time to search. The lies aren't going to be planned and will pile on top of each other. I need to see if you have any obvious ticks. Brick's a cop. He'd be able to tell."

Shit. He's right. I've been cautious, but Brick is a trained police officer and good enough at lying to convince us of his innocence these past few years, confirming his skills at deception. He would know if I'm lying if I'm not any good at it. Maybe I am skilled, or maybe Brick's intoxicated state last night gave me the upper hand.

"Okay." I bring my feet to the couch, crossing my legs and turning toward Kilo. I close my eyes and breathe, trying to think of a lie. I stare at him blankly. "My favorite food is seafood."

The corners of Kilo's lips upturn. "Okay. Now tell me something true."

"I've never been to Cancun."

His smile widens. "Okay, now another lie."

"I've never masturbated."

He bursts into a laugh as my cheeks heat. I don't know why I said that. Maybe I wanted to make him more uncomfortable by throwing him off, but I should have said anything else. There was no need to admit to this man I barely know that I touched myself. He's already caught me in enough embarrassing situations to last a lifetime.

He straightens, pointing a finger at me. "That's a good one. Thought you'd throw me off there."

"Did I?"

He shakes his head no. "I'll admit, you're not bad, but it's your pupils. They dilate when you lie."

"Really?"

"It's subtle, but if you do it enough and he catches on to the pattern, you're screwed."

I cover my eyes with my hands. "How do I make it stop?"

"Practice," he says as if it's the easiest thing in the world. "You need to lie more, and I'll watch and let you know when you're doing it. Once you realize, you'll start to correct the habit."

"Okay," I scoot closer, widening my eyes. "Let's do this." I puff out my chest, ready to become a lying master.

"Tell me things I wouldn't know about you, and I'll decide if you're lying or not."

"Okay." I try not to think too hard, rapid fire spewing random facts. "I don't like broccoli."

"Lie."

"I've never watched The Godfather?"

"Truth?" he questions.

"Yes."

"I..."

He holds up a hand. "Wait, you've never watched The Godfather?"

"No. Doesn't really seem like my jam."

"No, but you have to watch it."

"Right now?"

He chuckles. "Not right now, but later. It'll be a date." It's his turn for his cheeks to heat, and I can't help but grin. "Okay. Sorry, back on track. Keep going."

I don't notice I've scooted closer to him, and I shiver as our knees brush. "I am afraid of chickens."

"Lie."

"Ugh! How do I make my pupils not dilate?"

"The trick is, when you lie, it needs to be as close to the truth as possible. It'll make you less nervous." I'd be less nervous if he left the room. I'm also under intense scrutiny—making me even more readable than usual.

"Okay." I think for a moment. "I don't brush my teeth in the morning."

"Um, truth?" He cringes.

"Ha! Well, technically, I wait until after I eat breakfast. It's still the morning, but it's not the first thing I do."

Kilo nods and claps his hands. "Okay, okay. We're getting somewhere! Keep going!"

"I only eat steak medium rare."

"Truth?"

"Nope! I mean, I will, but I'll eat it other ways too."

I'm so thrilled by my improving abilities that I don't think clearly before opening my mouth and spewing the first thing that pops into my head. "I'm not attracted to you."

The air thickens, and the fucks I want to yell rest inside of my mouth. I study Kilo as his eyes widen, and he takes me in. "Lie," he replies, his eyes focused on my lips.

"Well, technically..."

"Technically?" How did he get so close to me? His breath whispers across my lips, his heat warming the small space between us.

My eyes close as he leans in, anticipating his lips on mine. "Please tell me you just mastered the skill of lying." His eyes close, the tension relying on my next action.

"Maybe," I whisper, my mind washing of reason.

"I guess I'll just have to test for myself." He removes the small distance, pressing his lips against mine and grabbing the back of my neck to hold me to him. I open, the breath I'd been holding leaving my mouth and filling his. Once he senses my willingness for the embrace, the kiss intensifies, and his other hand crawls up my back and pulls me toward him, directing me onto his lap. I crawl on, not breaking our kiss, my hands running over the expanse of his muscular back.

It's a good kiss. The slickness between my legs demands attention, but something is missing. His smell doesn't drive me wild, a crucial component for Weres. He could fuck me here on the couch, and it would be decent enough, but it would leave me wanting more. I need a distraction, though. A simple make-out session would be good for my head, but as his hands crawl up my front to grab my breasts, I freeze. He notices the hesitance, immediately pulling back and examining me before I crawl off his lap.

I deflate, kicking myself for ruining what could have been a simple relief. I'm assuming he's returning to his Nordic home one of these days. This could be uncomplicated and fun, but I've already ruined the moment by displaying discomfort. He smiles at me, brushing a strand of hair behind my ear. "So, can I assume you've gotten better at lying?"

I smile with a nod. "What can I say? I had a great teacher." I don't tell him the truth, hoping he doesn't notice my aversion to the question. Yes, I think Kilo is attractive, but the truth my mind settled on to deliver the convincing lie had everything to do with my overpowering, devastatingly annoying attraction to Brick.

13

PHONE HOG

My attendance at the office has been limited ever since Red's been on bed rest. Other people work at the Dayton Daily besides the two of us. We have an office manager, a bookkeeper, and an intern, but I'm not necessarily friends with them. They're all nice enough, but they're just coworkers, not people I'd want to chit-chat with. With Red absent, there's no pressing need to sit in my cubicle. I can work at home just as well.

It's Friday. Two days have passed since I last saw Brick. I'm itching to do more to help the pack now that my position is solidified. All I can do is wait for Brick to schedule another date. After how we left things, I'm nervous he'll prolong our next meeting. After all, he ran out of my house as fast as he could. I could easily text him, but it wouldn't be believable. My hatred toward him wasn't a secret. If I play too desperate too early, I'll blow everything. But then again, it's obvious he's also using me. He hated me, too. There's no reason for him to go on dates with me other than extracting information, and he clearly thinks he's doing it.

I wonder if he's suspicious of me since the Hunters were caught at Josie's house. Multiple women have gone missing or have been murdered, so it isn't surprising that we'd have Weres patrolling the area. Maybe he does know I set him up. I just have to hope he's willing to allow it again at the chance of snagging useful information from me. We're both playing a very complicated game.

I can't let myself stew in the uncertainty of all of this. Instead, I throw myself into my work, writing my big expose article revealing all of the Hunters' evil doings. When it's done, it will be riddled with evidence—police reports, pictures of their secret hideouts, mugshots of the guilty men. Obviously I don't have this information right now, but I write around it, making up what I think will be the ending. I type out a paragraph on Brick, naming him as a double agent for the Hunters, using his position to gain wealth and power promised by the evil group. It doesn't feel as good as I thought, calling him out for his shit. Maybe once I have the evidence, it will feel better.

As if the thought of Brick summons the demon himself, my phone lights up. It's a text from an unknown number. *Date this weekend?*

At first, I assume it's Brick, but then I remember I don't have Kilo's number. God, fooling around with two men on the same day sure has its consequences. It's a Dayton area code, but maybe Kilo's using a different number while he's here. I know shit about how international phone service works. If I texted Kilo under the impression he was Brick, he wouldn't be upset; this is what he trained me for, but I have to think of a clever way to respond. A thought pops into my mind. *Should we watch The Godfather?*

He's as quick a texter as he is at emailing. *What? The Godfather? No. Hate that movie.* Okay, so we've got Brick on the line. It was kind of an odd request, so I must recover. *Okay, just checking. I also hate that movie.* I mean, I probably would.

I have something else planned. No movie, he responds.

Shit. A movie at his place would be the perfect situation for some spying. We'd make out, fuck, I could get him drunk again, he'd pass out, and then I could snoop through his shit. The idea excites me more than it should. I want to protest, but I hesitate. Whatever he has planned could still work. A date could always end up back in his bed.

I didn't even say yes to the date. I might have plans.

You don't have plans.

How do you know? I have a very active social life, thank you very much.

If you had plans, you would have said that before mentioning The Godfather.

Maybe I made plans since you're stalling.

His reply doesn't return immediately, and I smile, assuming I bested him. My phone rings, and horror washes over me. He wants to have a phone call. Ew. I let it go to voicemail, but he immediately calls me again. I sigh and pick up. "What?"

"What? How about hello?"

"Why are you calling? And how the fuck did you even get my number?"

He scoffs. "I'm a Sergeant. I have my ways, and I'm trying to plan something with you. Your messages are cryptic as fuck. I just need to know if you're available tomorrow morning."

"It depends."

"Depends?"

"Yeah, depends on what you have in mind."

"Can't it be a surprise?"

Considering he's a potential murderer, no, but I don't say this. "Does it involve me getting hurt?"

He sighs. "Why would I bring you on a date where you get hurt?"

"I don't know. Your last date involved you getting hammered drunk and me having to carry your huge ass back to my house. You're lucky I'm a werewolf, or I'd never be able to manage."

His voice softens. "I know I'm sorry. I was just... nervous." He sounds sincere, and I feel bad for shitting on him. Only for a moment, though, and then I remember who he is. "I want to make it up to you, so I've planned something that will be fun and won't involve alcohol."

"Hmm." I want to make him squirm.

After a moment of silence, he clears his voice. "Besides, I didn't think the ending of our date was that horrible for you."

I'm frozen in shock. Did he just say what I thought he said? Yes, we're supposed to go on another date, and maybe I'm giving him a harder time than I should, but it's an unspoken rule that we don't bring up what happened in my bed. Especially for him since he left in such haste, obviously regretful. Does he think he can make me squirm, and I'll fold? He should know me better than that.

"It was clearly a good time for you," I reply.

"Clearly, but it could have been better." Okay, ouch. Sure, I didn't even touch his cock, but I'd like to think even my ass rubbing against his shaft was earth-shattering.

"What if that's the best you're going to get?" I reply.

"Is that what you want?"

"I don't know yet."

His voice is low, airy, and thick. "You screamed my name with just an ounce of my attention. Imagine the sounds I could pull from you with my cock buried deep inside of you." I pull the phone away from my ear, looking down at it with my mouth agape. There's no fucking way he just said that to me. Who does he think he is? I adjust myself, sitting crisscross on my bed. My wet panties grab my attention. I like this more than I should. I probably made him sweat enough. I returned the phone to my ear, listening to his breath on the other end.

"And you came just from the feel of me. If I let you fuck me, you'd never recover."

His voice shifts an octave lower. "Don't worry about me, little wolf. You won't catch me protesting if you want to ride me for hours."

I scoff even as my hand clenches outside my lounge shorts. "You wish."

"And you don't?"

"No." My voice holds no confidence.

"Then why are you straining to reach between your legs?" I whip my head around my room, my throat constricting. "Are you watching me right now?"

He laughs. "So you are tempted to touch yourself. You play a big game, Carmen, but I can always read you. Even now, I can feel your arousal through the phone."

"And what about you? I bet you're rubbing your hand over your cock, imagining my ass grinding against you," I say with annoyance.

"No, I'm imagining much more than that."

I rub at myself from the outside of my shorts. It's subconscious, and I hate myself for it, but his words make my body unable to control. "Like what?" I hate the question. Even as I try to mask it disdainfully, it comes out much too breathy.

"I'm imagining you straddling me, rubbing your velvet cunt up my length. Nearly getting off just from the texture of me."

"Can't even fuck me in your fantasies, huh?"

He tsks. "Carmen, real men don't fuck right away. I have to get you soft and malleable for me first, so you're squelching around my cock."

Somehow, my hand has made its way down my shorts and beneath my soaking underwear. I move slowly as if Brick can hear me if I pick up my pace. I don't want to give him the satisfaction of knowing what his oddly sensual words are doing to me. A heavy breath escapes me, and I clamp my lips, but it's too late. I can hear the smile on his stupid face. He goes on, "I'd let you slide over my dick until you can't take it anymore, clenching me in your small hands and positioning my swollen head at your entrance, but I'd pull you back."

I scoff, my fingers now circling my clit, annoyed but too aroused to do anything else.

He continues. "No, I won't let you ride my cock until you beg me to fuck you."

I laugh this time. "I'd never beg you. I won't have to."

"Oh, you sound so sure."

"If my cunt was anywhere near you, you'd come from the sight of it."

"Maybe," he offers. "But I can keep coming, little wolf." What the fuck is with his new nickname for me? I can't say I hate it. At least not right now, with my ecstasy mixing in with my hate. "I'd use my cum to help me fit. It won't be easy to sheath inside of you, but I'd make it work. I'd make it so good for you."

I'm lost now, unable to think of words, only moans leaving my lips. I've ended up on my back somehow, my fingers rubbing my sensitive bud without caution. My brain clouds with his words, imagining his hand down my panties.

"That's it. Moan for me. Just like that." I cry out, not letting up the pressure. "Oh, fuck." he whimpers, and I realize he's probably touching himself too. I have to know. "Where are your hands, Brick?" I ask.

"Wrapped around my cock."

I moan, my brain picturing him lounging in a dark room, his legs spread wide as he yanks himself from tip to base. I'd do anything to see him right now.

"God, Carmen. You'd feel so much better. I'd already been filling you by now."

My orgasm washes over me. I edged myself even to make it this long. I scream out, wringing out every last drop. Bricks moans echo in my ear, eliciting another wave of ecstasy.

Only a moment of silence passes between us as we catch our breaths. I wait for him to sputter apologies and hang up. Whenever he shows me any level of attraction, it seems to be against his will. But to my surprise, his commanding voice doesn't waver. "Don't make plans Sunday morning. I'll pick you up at ten." He hangs up. Leaving me sated, confused, and pissed the fuck off.

14

TRUFFLE PIG

en always think they're so clever whenever they propose a surprise date. It's sweet in theory, but in reality, it's annoying as shit trying to figure out what to wear. We could go deep sea scuba diving for all I know, and I could land on a ball gown. I settled on a pair of jeans, a tank top, and a cardigan. It's the morning, after all, so my ensemble shouldn't require any frills.

I stand in my driveway, arms crossed over my chest, and not letting amusement grace my face as Brick pulls in. He parks, giving a tight-lipped smile. I guess he's not opening the door for me. My stomach bundles at the thought of our conversation yesterday as I stomp to the passenger side and climb inside.

"Hello," I say, not brave enough to meet his eyes. He just nods as a greeting before backing out and driving down the road.

If I thought the car ride was awkward during our last date, I was gravely mistaken. The silence coating us brings a whole new meaning to the word uncomfortable. One minute, Brick is stoic and uncaring; the next, hate lights his eyes, and then bam, he turns into a dungeon Daddy and whispers dirty things into my ear and drags orgasms from me without even touching my skin. This must be one of the most infuriating things about Brick, and boy, there is a lot. I can't pretend it doesn't thrill me, but most of all, it makes me hate him even more. My secret spy seduction act fairs much more difficult with a target like Brick.

I can't take it anymore. After fifteen minutes, I break the silence. "Can I know where you're taking me now?"

He contemplates for a moment but finally says, "Olympic Park."

"Why so you can murder me and no one will hear me scream?" I'm only half kidding. My stomach flutters, thinking about being in such a remote location with him.

He deadpans. "You're a werewolf, Carmen. I think you'll be fine."

I study his side profile, ignoring the perfect slope of his nose or the too-thick eyelashes that no male should be blessed with. Does he really believe what he's saying? He's much stronger than me for some reason, and I doubt it's unknown to him. Of course, it's rude to ask people about their supernatural origins. In our culture, you wait for people to reveal themselves. After centuries of monster hunting and villagers running our kind out of town with torches and pitchforks, it leads to a very taboo topic. We're comfortable talking about it once it's shared, and we witness others in their other form. But until then, we keep our mouths shut.

I'm sick of niceties with Brick as if there was really any between us. "What are you exactly?"

He arches his neck in surprise and shoots me a look. "What am I?"

"Like, are you a Were?"

He clenches his fists on the steering wheel. "I thought it was obvious."

"I can't smell it on you."

"Probably because I bathe."

I chuckle. "Most Weres bathe, but I can still make out their scent."

He shrugs. "I don't know what to tell you."

"The truth?"

"I'm a Were, okay? But obviously, I'm not trying to tell the world."

Words lodge at the back of my throat. This is the sentiment of my pack, a way to keep us safe from the Hunters. Ironic coming from his lips. He must be a traitor to his own kind. I can't think of anything more pathetic. Anger lines my reserve. I'm supposed to lure him into my trap, but I can't help myself. "Must be nice to have a choice on whether or not people know about your powers." I cross my arms over my chest, letting my head rest against the window.

He's silent for a moment. "That must have been hard." I don't reply, but he continues. "Growing up without the protection that your brother had, but with all the risk."

"Cameron protected me," I reply, more childlike than expected.

"I imagine you protected yourself a lot of the time." The words wash over me. It's true. I know this already—I have come to terms with it, even if it results in my callus exterior and drive to live fully without caution. I never know when it will be my turn to be overtaken by the Hunters. "Sometimes, I think I'm the fortunate one. I've survived out in the open. Others haven't been so lucky in the shadows." I drill my gaze into him, trying to catch something—remorse, hatred, anything.

He nods, his chest deflates, and his eyes take on a somber look. "It won't be like this forever."

"How do you know?"

"You might not think your words do much, but your exposés bring powerful people and their wrongdoings to light. With all of us working together, this will end."

"But it's worse now than ever before. Women are being taken and murdered."

"It'll end." He takes his eyes off the road, staring into mine as if trying to deliver a message. There's weight to his words and sadness behind his eyes. He's a traitor. He's proved this on multiple occasions, but staring at him now makes me feel like I've got something wrong and missing something.

"Shit," he says, yanking his wheel just before he misses the turn to the National Park entrance. I'm rocked sideways but straighten myself once we bump along the dirt road leading to the park parking lot.

"What are we doing here?" I bark once he turns the car off.

"Jesus Christ, you are not fun to surprise." He slams the door behind him, moving toward the backseat.

"I don't know what gave you the idea I would be." A mosquito bites my neck and pisses me off even more. I'm a creature of the woods. It's not like I don't enjoy outside activities; I just don't feel particularly sexy surrounded by bugs, and I need all the sexy voodoo I can get for this date.

Brick walks toward the entrance of the woods, a picnic basket in hand. My heart softens a bit at the sight of him, even as he carries on without turning around to see if I'm following. He planned a picnic for us? I can't deny the thought pulls at my heartstrings and dampens my panties. I kick the attitude as I follow him, eager to discover more about his role in this mystery and learn about the man behind the brick exterior.

"Have you ever been mushroom foraging before?" he asks once I've caught up with him. Fractured light bursts through the canopy of leaves overhead, and songbirds call in the distance.

"Nope."

"Well, I thought I'd teach you how to look for mushrooms." He points to his nose. "I've got a gift for smelling out the best 'shrooms.'"

I cross my arms over my chest. "Wow, how nice of you to take me on a date where you teach me something," I say sarcastically but smile to let him know I'm only half serious.

He rolls his eyes and cocks his head. "I know. Very mansplainy of me to do, but I thought it could add to the picnic, and it would be a fun activity to get to know each other better."

"Get to know each other better? I didn't think you'd be interested in that."

He stops, turning to me and catching me off guard. He grabs me with his free hand, his expression serious. "I like you, Carmen."

My heart speeds. "You like me?" I internally smack myself for letting my bones turn to mush. I don't need this man's approval, but why do I want it so badly?

He scoffs with a smile. "Obviously. This is our second date."

"You could have ulterior motives." It's a stupid thing to say. I could completely blow my cover, but I must see him respond to the comment.

"If anything, it benefits me more to stay away from you." He continues walking, stopping when something catches his eye, and crouches to search through the foliage.

"How so?"

He picks a mushroom and scrutinizes it. "It's incredibly dangerous for me to be with you." He straightens, and his eyes widen as if just releasing words he should have been guarding.

"Why is it dangerous to be with me?" I step closer to him, examining him.

He brushes off the dirt from his prize mushroom and throws it into his basket. "You distract me."

"How so?" I hate that I'm stopping and starting whenever this man decides to make a move, as if he knows I'll keep following him around.

"Well, instead of reading reports yesterday when I was working from home, I was talking to you and jerking myself off."

"Brick!" I yell.

"What?" He gives me a confused glance before squatting down again to capture another mushroom.

"You can't say that kind of stuff out loud." My cheeks beat bright. Not from the weather, it's surprisingly cool in the shade, but from this man's unfiltered words.

He looks around, wiping the dirt off his little fungi. "We are alone in the woods."

"Yeah, but it's the middle of the day. Those words are meant only to be said in a very particular setting."

"So you don't fuck in the middle of the day?"

I give a sharp laugh. "Who said anything about fucking?"

He steps toward me, all attention off his stupid mushroom, and directed toward me. "You said those words aren't meant for the middle of the day. If I fucked you right here, I'd probably mention how often I jerk off, wishing it was you wrapped around my cock."

He's a menace. Thank fucking God he's hot, or I'd shit my pants. He says this sentence confidently, with no hesitation in his words. Suddenly, space doesn't exist between us. His lips are only centimeters away from mine. My nipples are hard and sensitive, eager to step forward and brush against his chest covered by a flannel shirt. I close my eyes, ready to surrender.

"Let's stop pretending this is something that it's not." I open my eyes to catch him staring down at me, heat behind his gaze. The air from my lungs disappears when he steps away, brushing past me and crouching near a bush.

I clench my eyes shut, stilling my mind, willing my cunt to stop gushing and cursing myself for letting Brick distract me yet again. Yes, I can't smell the Were on Brick. It's subtle, but there is something there—powerful and earth-shattering. It's unlike any scent I've ever encountered, and I blame it completely for my inability to behave rationally around him.

I stand in the silence for a moment longer, Brick still rustling around behind me. His words ring through me: *Let's stop pretending this is something that it's not.* There's so much he could mean. Is this more? Is this exactly what I expected all along—us both playing a very complicated and dangerous game? There's only one way to find out.

I shake the fog away, turning and pressing my palms against my hips. "You said you were going to teach me about mushroom foraging, but you haven't taught me shit."

He pops to his feet, presenting a cluster of delicate brown caps. "These are oyster mushrooms."

I move in closer, peering into his dirt-encrusted hands. "How do you know?"

He shrugs. "From the way that they look."

I scrunch my face. "Wow, you're an excellent teacher."

He laughs, the rare sound knocking me off-kilter. "Yeah, I don't know why I thought I could teach you. I actually don't know anything. It's just instinctual." With that, he tosses the mushroom in his bag and walks onward, leaving me in the dust.

"Did you grow up on a mushroom farm?" I ask, rushing up to him, yet again. Thank God, I'm in good shape, or I'd be completely out of breath from chasing him around.

"No." Nothing else.

"No?"

"I did not grow up on a mushroom farm." Silence, except the snapping of twigs under-toe.

"Jesus Christ, Brick. It's literally like talking to a brick wall."

"What?" His face reads genuine confusion.

"I ask you questions, and you reply with one-word answers. Don't ask me anything about myself. Have you ever had a conversation in your life?" This is one thing I enjoy about being with him. Yes, he's horrible at conversation, but let's be honest, most men are. At least I can call him out on his crap.

He sighs. "I'm sorry. I don't have a lot of conversations that aren't business-related. I'm not great at socializing."

"You don't have any friends?"

He contemplates. "Not really. I moved here three years ago and was thrown into my role."

"Does that bother you?"

"Not really. I grew up as an only child, so I'm used to it."

His childhood. This could lead to where things all went wrong. The light shifts as we leave the woods, soft, plush grass before us. A creek sings below the cliff's edge—a postcard view. Brick walks toward the green lip overlooking the creek, placing his basket down and pulling out a checkered blanket.

I don't let the topic pass us by. "Where did you grow up?"

"New York City."

"Wow! I can't imagine living somewhere without the cover of the woods nearby." As an adolescent Were, shifting is less voluntary. Living near the woods helps us hide our true selves during the transition period.

He huffs with a forced smile. "Yeah, it was shit. It didn't help that I had no idea what was happening."

"Your parents didn't tell you?" My parents were killed by Hunters when Cameron and I were young, but I still had the privilege of their guidance for a few of my adolescent years. I know many Weres aren't so lucky.

"It was just my mom. My dad was a one-night stand; she had no idea he was a Were. When I started showing signs, she took me to the doctor. Luckily, living in such a big city made the medical community aware of the paranormal. They set me up with a doctor who specialized in my abilities and gave me resources. I probably wouldn't be here today if it weren't for them. I think that's why I joined the National Department of Supernatural the minute I graduated college."

I'm so distracted by his story that I barely register him setting up two green mats, wooden plates, and unwrapping two cut sandwiches to place atop his presentation. He says these words so easily, almost without thought, as he works on setting up his picnic. It must be accurate, but he could very well be leaving out the details of the Hunters getting to him first and influencing him to work to help them. It would be easier for someone without any Were family. The Hunters could make him feel like he was different, destined to help eradicate the kind that brought him into this world and did nothing to help his upbringing. But even with this consideration, I can't help but feel for him. This calloused man, so alone in this world from the start, loves foraging mushrooms and setting up intricate picnics complete with a vase flower centerpiece.

He takes a breath, examining his display, straightening the bowl of grapes before turning his gaze to me. Wind sweeps around us, blowing my hair from my shoulders. He sniffs and groans. I used to think my smell repulsed him, but the look on his face right now isn't pain like before; it's pure admiration.

A thick silence washes over us, peaceful yet riddled with electricity, exposed wires ready to catch flame to everything around us. I break the quiet before it becomes too much. "Wow, this is quite a set up."

He blinks rapidly, coming back to reality. "Oh, I almost forgot." He reaches into the basket and places a handful of his newly retrieved mushrooms on each of our plates.

I scoot closer to my spot, examining the mushroom. "How do I know this isn't a poisonous mushroom?"

"Like I would purposely poison you?"

"Maybe." I shrug, dangling a small piece of the oyster mushroom over my lips.

"What a convoluted way to kill you."

I laugh this time, eliciting a jerk from him, as if the noise of my laughter pulled something from his chest. "Fine, maybe it wouldn't be on purpose, but explaining that you know what type of mushroom this is *because of the way that they look,* doesn't give me the most confidence."

He sighs and shakes his head, a small smile on his lips. "Fine, I'll eat it first, and then if I'm alive in twenty minutes, you can eat it."

"Hm, I don't know about that. What if you poison yourself, and I have to drag you to the emergency room? I don't have it in me to lug you around for two dates."

He swallows the mushroom. "You're so difficult."

"Yes, but you love it."

"Unfortunately, yes." How did I get so close to him again? We're both sitting with our legs outstretched in opposite directions, our faces nearly inches apart. He stops chewing, zoning in on my lips.

"What else do you love about me?" I smirk, trying to cut the tension nearly drowning us.

He resists my attempts, reaching out and placing his thumb on the center of my lip. "I'd be unable to stop if I started."

My chest heaves, and my eyes flutter, yet still, I try to carry on. "I've got time."

"Words aren't my strong suit. I'd rather show you." He leans in, kissing me softly. Every nerve in my body sizzles. It's so sweet, yet so much more. The sweetness only lasts a second, and he whimpers against my mouth as his other hand scoops the back of my neck, pressing me hard against him. Brick always gives all his attention to his current task—from examining a crime scene to foraging mushrooms. This kiss is all of him. I can feel every corner of his brain honing in on me.

I moan into his mouth, and he growls at the arousal radiating from my lips. His lips travel across my jaw, moving to my earlobe. "I love your lips," he whispers into my ears.

I smile, wrapping my arms the best I can around his huge torso, needing him closer. "I love the words that come out of them. I love the way they look—the way they feel."

"Really? I thought my words were the first thing to irritate you."

"Yes, but it makes my dick so hard when you're a brat." He grabs my hand, placing it on his hardened cock under his jeans. I already feel the moisture of his precum slipping through the fabric.

"Kinky, Brick," I tease.

"Only for you." He presses forward, pushing me onto my back and holding himself over me, his lips and hands not leaving me. His touch travels down my neck, pawing at my breasts covered by my t-shirt. "I love your tits," he says into my mouth.

"I thought you said words weren't your strong suit," I say around his rough kisses. I don't want him to stop telling me everything he loves about me, but he did mention he loves it when I'm a brat. Gotta keep that dick of his hard if I want it to ruin me the way my cunt begs for.

"They're not, but I smell the arousal thickening on you whenever I encourage you. Gotta keep that cunt wet and juicy before I devour it."

Goddamn, this man.

His hand trails down my chest, over my stomach, and pushes between my jeans and underwear, finding the heat of my core. "Fuck." He pulls away from my mouth, clenching his eyes.

"Going to come in your pants again just from the feel of me?" I smirk.

He turns his attention back to me, eyes blazing, tracking every inch of my face. His mouth opens with a moan as he inserts a finger inside of me. I cry out. "Let's see who's coming first this time. You feel so ready." He inserts another finger, stretching me as his thumb presses against my clit. I'm completely clothed, and I'm about to sputter out of control.

He doesn't return his lips to mine, watching me as if I'm one of the world's wonders as he fucks me with his fingers. His gaze is too intense, mixed in with the powerful sensation between my legs—I can't keep my eyes open.

He stops his movements. "Eyes on me, little wolf," he orders, no humor in his voice. I pop them open, even if they are heavy the moment he continues inserting himself. I don't let them close, though, watching him moan and groan with each of my whimpers. He's so responsive to my arousal, clenching his teeth and shutting his eyes every few seconds to steady himself. I try my best to hold out. He appears so close to his edge, and if I'm anything, it's competitive.

But then he pulls some bullshit, curling his fingers and rubbing at the spongy spot behind my clit. My orgasm washes over me like a thermal spring, surprising me as it floods my nervous system.

"Oh, such a good girl," he says, eyes not leaving mine. "Take all of it. Don't hold anything back." He continues his pressure, my pussy squelching from his fingers.

I relax momentarily, closing my eyes and catching my breath. Brick falls over me, kissing down my neck. Goosebumps immediately pepper my skin, and a new wave of moisture floods my already soaking panties. "I won," he whispers, and I push him back, startling him, but once I work at the buttons of his flannel, he softens, helping me in my attempt to undress him. He may have won, but right now, I don't fucking care. I'm too set on watching him come that I'll worry about him bragging later.

He sits up, ripping the shirt off his frame once it's halfway unbuttoned. I nearly come again from the sight of him. I could feel his muscles and witness their shape under his clothes, but goddammit, he's beautiful. "Are you shitting me?"

"What?" He tries to play coy, but the cocky smirk gives it away.

"Why do you look like that? There's no reason to have those abs."

He pushes me back, ripping off my pants in one powerful pull at the hem. His fingers push aside my lacy panties, and he groans, stroking his finger through me. "The working out is worth something. You're so fucking wet."

I don't know how he can think of the most diabolical words. I can't think of anything except his dick inside of me. I wrap my arms around his neck, trying to pull his lips to mine, but he pulls back, trailing kisses down my neck. He pulls my shirt and bra overhead so he can continue kissing my chest, licking at my nipples and grinding against me.

"God, are you going to fuck me already?" I yell, needing more from him. I've already orgasmed it's time to be properly fuck.

He reaches for my cunt, his lips still on my nipples, before pulling away. "I've got a big cock, little wolf. I need you even wetter than this to take me."

"I'll believe it when I see it." I've only ever felt his cock grinding against my ass or my stomach while he's completely clothed. I know it's going to be huge—*my pussy will take forever to recover* huge—but I need to see it first to prepare mentally.

"Soon," he says between kisses down my stomach, climbing between my pants and pulling down my panties. I'm officially buck-ass naked in the middle of the national park. This is a felony, I'm sure of it, but I think I could get out of it. I do have the head office pig between my legs, after all.

He breathes over my cunt, his breath quivering. "God, your fucking smell—it's so delicious. I think I might come just from the taste." He swipes me gently with his tongue, sending my body into a shivering mess. "So fucking good," he groans, before spreading my lips with his fingers, lapping me with eager strokes. His tongue is large and massages every inch of my cunt. He licks as if this is more for his enjoyment than my own, but holy fuck is it good. Something about an eager pussy eater makes any technique absolutely exquisite.

I'm so close to my edge again, but he pulls back with a hiss–turning his head to the side and clamping his eyes. "God, I'm close."

I push myself up, crawling toward him and shoving him to the soft green grass. "My turn," I say as I un-button his jeans, and he helps me pull them down his monstrous thighs. His cock is full-mast underneath his cotton boxer briefs, and when I pull them down, he pops free—gloriously long and thick with healthy veins running to the tip. My mouth waters at the sight of him, but my hands itch to explore him. I cup his balls, the weight heavy and full. I gasp, catching his eyes. "Never seen a knot before?" He studies me curiously.

"I have, just surprised." Not all Weres have knots. Some only have them visible when in the presence of their mate, and some, the rarer, have them all the time. The latter is usually for males that never have a mate, and instead, nature insists on using them to breed the whole fucking world. Brick must be the second type of Were. Obviously. I don't even entertain the alternative. It's fine with me if he knots me; in fact, it makes me even wetter, if that's even possible.

Female Weres have the kick-ass ability to control when we want to be pregnant. We still ovulate and menstruate as human woman, but we have the supernatural ability to stop sperm in their track with our mental abilities. It's kind of like Red's mental powers except on a minuscule level. I've heard of some females who thought they didn't want a baby, but subconsciously, they did, and their brains took control of their true desires, but that won't be a problem for me. There's no way I want a child right now. That's for sure.

"We can stop," Brick says, catching his breath and clearly in physical pain at the thought.

"We're not fucking stopping." I bring my lips to his tip and circle his head with my tongue.

"Jesus fucking Christ," he cries, falling completely to his back. He bites the back of his hand as I roll my lips down his shaft.

His visceral response makes me eager. I take him fully, hitting the back of the throat. I ignore my gags, slurping him up and down, wanting him to lose control—this man is so stoic and reserved, brick-like, you could say, but melts like a popsicle from my touch. I cup his balls with one hand, and with the other, I twist at the bottom of his shaft. Even going all the way to the back of my throat isn't enough to take all of him.

Just when I'm really getting into it, my cunt throbbing at his breathy moans and the subtle jerks from his hips, he pushes me back. I catch myself on my elbows, staring at him in disbelief. He moves over me, pushing me to the ground, and positions his head at my cunt. "I can't take it anymore." He drives into me, hard and rough, forcing a cry of pain mixed with pleasure from my throat. "You infuriate me, even with your lips around my cock, and yet, I can't stop wanting you." He grits his teeth as he fucks me, his hot breath at my neck.

His words ring true. I should hate this man. Although doubt lines my theories of him as a traitor to his kind and the culprit of my people's demise, he's the enemy. He's my target. Yet I can't keep my hands off him. My mind won't stop playing images of him fucking me just like this.

With each thrust, he deepens, until I'm stretched by his half-hardened knot, applying pressure at my entrance with the most delicious pain. His body tenses over me, and he moans low in his throat. I don't close my eyes, watching as he slowly transforms before my eyes. His nose and ears elongate, fur coating his growing body. It's not a complete shift, but something strikes me as odd. There's a unique characteristic to his half-form.

I feel my own transformation happening as well. Odd since I'm usually in control of my shifts, even on the brink of ecstasy. I ignore it though, letting my claws slightly dig into his back.

He attempts to pull back at the last moment, clearly not wanting to knot me. I focus all my strength on keeping him pressed against me. "You sure?" he barely gets out.

"Knot me, Brick." The words send him over the edge. He thrusts into me harder than the rest, sending a rush of cum inside of me. His knot expands, hardening and trapping me to him. His cum doesn't stop, filling me until I nearly feel it at the back of my throat. My second orgasm washes over me, the pain turning my body into a sputtering mess. It takes longer than usual for us to settle, my mind finally clearing and my sweat-covered body relaxing into the picnic blanket underneath me. Brick buries his face into the crook of my neck, holding himself up so as not to crush me. His form is still massive, but I watch as the light fuzz sucks back into his skin—his body returning to its full human state. We'll be trapped like this until his knot deflates, but strangely, I don't mind the pressure of him.

Birds chirp in the distance, and the sun shines just behind a light veil of clouds. My eyes widen, taking in the scenery I've been blind to, my senses tunneling into Brick and blocking out everything else. A few flies loom over our untouched sandwiches beside us. "The food."

"What?" Brick mumbles against my skin.

"You put so much work into setting this up, and we didn't even eat."

He holds himself up on his forearms, giving me a scrunched-face look. "Carmen." He shakes his head. "Fuck the food." He brings his lips to my skin, kissing down my neck as if he's starved just for me. I let my head roll back, my skin already flushing with goose-bumps, my cunt already dampening. This man. He'll be the death of me for sure.

15

HOG-TIED

I'm the worst fucking spy on the planet. If this was a paid gig and not a generational duty, I'd be fired. Instead of insisting that Brick bring me back to his place so I could snoop through his shit while he slept, I let him return to my home. I didn't even protest when he pulled into my driveway and followed me inside. I just wrapped my arms around his thick neck and shoved my tongue down his throat. I let him pick me up by my ass, carry me to my bed, and fuck and knot me a few more times before falling asleep in his arms.

We both woke in a clearer state of mind. Although I would have enjoyed it if he rolled me over and shoved his face between my legs again, he just kissed me softly down my neck before dressing and slipping out the front door.

I'm supposed to report to Grimm about what I discovered during our second date. What can I possibly tell him? It's time to head back to the office. I can feign being too busy to talk if I'm not at home, vegging in my jammies for the sixth day in a row.

I quickly shower and dress, reveling in the soreness between my legs. I slap my cheek whenever I catch myself grinning, remembering Brick's words, the heat in his eyes, the way he looked completely naked. I'm not the type of girl to have my mind altered after being dicked down. I see men for who they are and can compartmentalize their abilities in bed and who they are as a person. I've slept with plenty of douches, i.e. Wood: culprit numero uno.

When a car pulls out in front of me on the way to the office, I don't even flip them off. I just huff and continue thinking about the way Brick ate the tiny sandwiches he prepared for me yesterday. How can he be so intense and so adorable at the same time? No! I slap myself. "Cut it out, Carmen!" I yell as I pull my car into my parking lot, swinging my laptop bag over my shoulder and searching for my office keys. Maybe it's the whole knotting thing. It's not the first time I've been knotted, but I've never had someone so eager about it or filled me so completely. I never thought knotting was my cup of tea, but with Brick, God, it's the whole damn kettle.

More than that, there's a shift in my intuition about him. I was sure he was working with the Hunters, but now I'm conflicted. He didn't say or do anything to reveal otherwise. Well, that's not true. When he told me that the animosity and fear within our community would end soon, his eyes told a story his mouth wouldn't share. Could he be inside of this thing deeper than I expected? Or is he just playing his role a little too well? He is the police, after all, trained to lie and get people to do what they want.

I flip the fluorescent lights on, and the silence of the empty office building fills the room. I'm early, and most people don't show up until after ten—relaxed office rules and all. This is good. There are no distractions, and I can throw myself into my work to stop my Brick hamster wheel brain from spinning.

I open my laptop, plug it into my monitor, and check my planner to see what to dive into first. There are a few stories I'm supposed to follow up on with sources. One about the closing of a family-owned grocery store, one about a racist statue continuing to be vandalized in the park. They would both lead to interesting pieces and be a welcomed reprieve from the madness of Hunters and werewolves. Instead of opening my email and sending a message to the contacts listed, I open Google.

Just as I suspect, nothing comes up when you look for Bryce Brick. Nothing except his picture and title under the Dayton Police Force website. It's unfair that he can look me up, and I can't do the same. The internet is a never-ending chasm. Maybe if I focused my search on his past, I'd discover more. I type in Bryce Brick and New York City. It's not the first link, but after a few scrolls, my cursor lands on an obituary. Not Brick's, thank God. This would be even more confusing if I'd fucked a dead guy, or more realistically, someone with a fake identity—although, it wouldn't surprise me. The obituary belongs to Margaret Brick, who died three years ago and is survived by her son, Bryce Brick.

My heart tugs at the corners. This isn't the news I wanted to find. He mentioned his mother yesterday, but he didn't say anything about her dying. I knew he was lonely, but now I know he doesn't have a single person in this world. Did he move to Dayton for a fresh start? Could he really be as innocent as a grieving son taking up a new post to get away from his painful memories?

"Carmen?"

I scream, whipping around. Claws shoot from my fingertips, and my fangs burst through my gums.

"Woah, I didn't mean to frighten you!" Grimm holds up his hands in defense.

I deflate, shifting back to my human form and catching my breath. "What the fuck are you doing here?"

He steps closer. "You haven't been picking up your phone. I needed to make sure you were okay." Concern etches across his face. He's still handsome, but the lines near his eyes and lips appear heavier. I'm unsure if it's from his worry about me or the entire pack. Probably the latter. I don't envy his position.

I rummage through my bag, pulling out my phone riddled with blaring notifications from Grimm.

"I didn't want to worry your brother, so I thought I'd look for you myself. I'm sorry, I didn't mean…"

"No, no. I'm sorry." I'd been so selfish. I didn't want to face my failures to a man I respected, so instead, I worried him enough to search for me across town. "I've just been behind on work and wanting to catch up on some articles."

His eyes dart to my computer screen, the obituary still pulled up. I don't need to frantically click out of my browser as if I've been caught. I'm a reporter. This webpage could very well be a part of my job, but my guilt takes over my reason. I'm more invested in Brick than I want to share.

Grimm takes a seat at a chair in the corner of my cubicle. "Well, you're alive. That's good news."

"Yes. I'm fine."

"Did you discover anything? Tell me what happened."

My cheeks heat, and he notices it right away. He shakes his head. "You don't need to tell me everything. I won't judge you for how you get information out of him, but I need to know if you uncovered something, no matter how minor it is."

I hadn't prepared to talk to him today. I have no lies to give him. I could tell him about the information I discovered about his mother and how I'm attempting to discover if it ties to his connection with the Hunters, but it feels wrong. Brick didn't even share with me about his mother's death. He's supposed to be the enemy, but I can't help but feel protective of this information.

I ball my fists at my lap. "I wasn't able to discover anything yesterday. It was a short date."

His thick eyebrow raises. "A short date?"

"Yes. He's not much of a talker and brought me home afterward." All true information. Maybe Kilo's training did come in handy.

He sighs, rubbing at his temple. "Carmen, we had eyes on you. We saw Brick leave your house this morning."

I jump to my feet, my blood rising in temperature. "Why did you pretend that you were worried about me being alive if you've had people watching me?" I snatch my bag, wanting to dart out of my office and away from this confrontation.

He stands, his hands pleading. "I wanted to see what you would say when asked. I meant it when I said I wouldn't judge you on how you retrieve information, but having Brick sleep at your place and lying about your time together causes me to be concerned."

"So what? Am I under investigation now? I'm doing this for the greater good. You know I hate Brick." The words feel hot and nasty on my tongue.

"Carmen, I trust you. I'm thankful for your continued help. I just want to know what's going on. I want to know that you're safe."

I extend my arms, turning in a circle. "I look safe to you, don't I?"

"Then why are you hiding things from me? I'm worried he's getting to you."

I move toward the exit of my office. "You should know me better and trust my judgment." I move past him. He's being irrational and maybe I'm running a bit too hot and should just share my doubts about Brick's involvement with the Hunters. I don't have any concrete evidence against it, though, just a vague intuition that could very well be caused by being superbly dicked down. I know this. I need to get out of here. We shouldn't have this conversation now.

"Carmen, I'm sorry. Let's talk about this," he calls after me.

I hold the front door for him to exit. I need to lock up and can't storm off dramatically. I sigh, meeting his saddened eyes. "I don't want to discuss this now. Give me some time to clear my head and work out some theories. I need to know you trust me enough to do that."

He stops in front of me. "I do trust you. Of course, I do."

I nod. "Good. I'll call you tonight."

He nods, walking to his red Porsche and hopping inside. I watch him drive out of the desolate parking lot before retrieving my keys and locking the door. So much for getting work done. It seems I need to spend more time clearing my head about Brick. I sigh, looking down at my bag as I walk to my car. Someone steps in front of me, startling me and sending me back a step. Before I have time to register the person, a hand wraps around my mouth, pressing a cloth over my airway. I only struggle against the masked stranger's grasp for a moment before my world turns dark, and my body limps.

16

LAB PIG

A beep drags me out of an endless darkness. I've had my fair share of blackout nights, requiring me to investigate before understanding where I fell asleep, and at first, I think this must be my situation. I don't remember drinking too much, but no one ever does immediately after they come to. Bright fluorescent lights needle their way into the thin skin of my eyelids, and I cover my eyes with my hands, slowly bringing them away as the pain lessens.

I sit before taking in the room around me. My neck and back hurt like a bitch, probably due to the cold tiled floor underneath me. I open my eyes, examining the sterile white room. White tiles cover every inch, and a metal cot with thin white bedding sits in the corner, parallel to a metal toilet.

Panic washes over me. I rise to my feet, cursing as I wobble, but my fear steadies me, and I approach the white door, attempting to turn the handle. It's locked, of course. I pound against the surface, screaming for someone to let me out. This reaction is purely instinct, not based on any intelligence. Memories drip into my brain about where I was last before I blacked out.

I attempt to shift, hair rising at my arms and my ears elongating, but I'm still woozy from the drugs and unable to change completely. It wouldn't matter anyway. As I walk the perimeter of the small room, pounding and kicking at every surface, I realize there's no way out, even for a werewolf.

I flip my cot over. It's stupid; there won't be a hidden set of keys underneath, but my panicked brain must assess every nook and cranny in this room before accepting defeat. When I'm about to curl into a ball and cry, the door clicks, and I flip to the source, using all my skills to bare my claws.

In walks two men in all black wearing heavy-duty vests over their chests. Their expressionless faces and the batons topped with coil wire in their hands give away their status. They're security, the muscle of whatever's happening here.

"You must calm down, Carmen. You're going to hurt yourself," says a familiar voice behind the mass of muscle. The two men part, revealing Kilo wearing a white lab coat, his hair gelled back more than usual, and an alarmingly smug smile plastered across his handsome features.

"Kilo, what the fuck?" I step toward him, and the men's batons burst to life, revealing electricity in the coils.

Kilo steps forward, unafraid of me, as he walks around my perimeter. It outrages me, but I don't want to react rashly. Curiosity controls all my attention. He sighs. "Must I spell it out for you?"

"Why don't you humor me? It seems you locked me in a cage. It's the least you can do."

He sighs, taking a seat on my bed. "For your pack's star warrior, I'd thought you'd catch on sooner. It seems your brother did when he fed me the information about that girl being home alone and not sharing that it was a set-up meant for Brick."

So it wasn't Brick who informed the Hunters. I can't help that my heart soars at this news. I'm locked in a cage, still feeling the effects of drugs, and yet all I can focus on is my elation that Brick isn't working against the pack. Kilo's words bring me back to reality. "I think this is penance enough for his trickery." I can only hope Cameron doesn't know about my capture. Of course, I want my freedom, but Red's due any day. He needs to focus on her.

"So what? You're a traitor to your own race? Working with the Hunters because you hate yourself?"

He laughs, shaking his head, sitting at the edge of my cot. "Would you fault someone born with an incurable disease, one that causes uncontrollable rage and to behave like an animal? If that person dedicated their whole life to ensuring no one would suffer the same fate, would you not call them a hero?"

"Being a werewolf is not a disease."

He stands, circling me again. "You and your people are confined to solitude, feared by masses, unable to control your primal urges during periods of the year."

"I have always been able to control myself just fine."

Kilo removes the distance between us, tracing the underside of my chin. "You sniff people. You behave like a dog. A pretty dog, but a dog nonetheless." I snap at his finger, my fangs beared. He moves away from me faster than humanly possible because, of course, he's not a human. "There you go, proving my point again." Rage boils in my blood, but I have an ounce of my wits left. I can't just attack him blindly. He's also a werewolf, one without drugs running through his veins. He could overtake me in a second. I need to play this strategically.

"I didn't choose to be a werewolf," he drones on, walking around me with his hands behind his back. "I was cursed with this affliction and have decided to dedicate my life to eradicating this disease. But there's only one way to do that: kill the existing werewolves."

"Why don't you just kill yourself? Help everyone in this world."

He sneers. How could I ever have thought of him as handsome? Of course, I know the truth now, and I didn't before, but looking at him makes me want to vomit. Imagining his lips on me turns my stomach cold. "I've thought about it," he replies. "Hunters raised me, brought me into this world for my powers to be used to stop werewolves' terror. There were many times I wanted to die." A sadness slips into his eyes, an emotion I don't think he meant for me to catch. "But I was smart. I knew my existence could bring good to this world instead of evil. I could use my powers and intelligence to think of a different solution for killing werewolves instead of procreating with them. Do you know how long we have to drug females to get them pregnant? It's quite annoying with your anti-pregnancy abilities."

I don't reply, knowing he'll continue with his evil villain plans regardless. My theories are correct. "I conducted experiments, devoted my life to finding a way to transfer the power, and finally, I got it." He smiles, stepping toward me. "Don't you want to know how?"

"I'm imagining you're going to tell me anyway." I want to sit down, my head swimming and the initial adrenaline that propelled me through my prison wearing off, but I straighten my spine, ready for the information this idiot will give me.

"I developed a drug using the menstrual blood of female Weres." He's giddy, as if waiting ages to brag about his brilliant discovery.

"What the fuck?"

He waves his hand. "Yes, it's quite annoying that we must keep them prisoners and collect their menstruation only once a month. I'd much prefer to drain and dump them, but it leads to a more plentiful supply. You bunch put up quite a fight, though. Some of your kind didn't take too kindly to being kidnapped and, as you know, ended up dead."

I don't have a rebuttal. I just stare at him in disbelief. They're taking our period blood? As if they weren't psychotic enough before. "I'm sorry." I shake my head, holding my temple. "Why are you taking our period blood?"

"It's the main ingredient in my serum. The molecular composition of your menstruation can be transferred to humans to give them the powers of Weres without the nasty side effects. Now, we don't need to reproduce with werewolves to use them as weapons. We can be our own weapons and eradicate werewolves for good."

I scoff. "You need therapy." That's the understatement of the year.

Someone opens the prison door, poking their head inside. "Sir, he's here."

"Excellent," Kilo responds, clapping his hands together in glee. "Bring him in. This will be good."

This will not be good. It's evident from the giddy smile on Kilo's face. "I must say, it hurt my feelings that you weren't as attracted to me as Brick. Not that I'd want to partake in fucking a dog, but you do have an alluring quality about you."

"Do you vomit when you jerk yourself off?" I ask through gritted teeth.

His eyes roam over me, disdain and disgust that he kept so well hidden all this time. He flicks his gaze to the door. "Ah, welcome!"

I stare at the staggeringly tall man in the doorway, taking in every inch of him, wanting to scream his name. Brick doesn't look at me, though. He just meets his gaze to Kilo's.

Kilo approaches him, slapping him on the back. It's then I notice that he's not in chains or guarded. My heart drops. Just when I thought Brick could have been wrongly accused, reality barrels through me. I felt something between us, something I'd never experienced. I had let myself get too deep, just like Grimm warned. I was sure that Brick must have felt the same way, too, but now he stands at the entrance of my prison, not even able to meet me in the eye.

Kilo glares at me with a smile, hand still on Brick's shoulder. "Here she is! I told you. There's no way she's getting out. No need to worry."

Brick nods, looking anywhere but at me. My eyes assess every inch of him, willing to stop the tears from leaving my eyes. I hope there's a tiny sign of an alternative reality, but he gives me nothing. He's as stoic as his name suggests.

My shoulders sag. My will to resist, to fight, leaves me. The feeling shocks me. I've never been a romantic, never been dependent on a man. Brick isn't even mine. He never was. I shouldn't feel such betrayal. I shouldn't. But it's like something old and foreign in me cracks open, sucking up my last ounce of hope.

I let the tear slide down my cheek, even as I clench my jaw to prevent me from crumbling.

Kilo catches it. He slaps Brick's chest. "My, my, Brick. You must pack an impressive package. It seems you got this hard cookie to crumble. You'll have to show me later. I'd love to see that."

Brick's mask falls. He steps away, anger lining his features. "That's disgusting." He's right. What Kilo suggests is repulsing, but I know his words are directed at me.

Kilo moves his hand to Brick's back, leading him toward the door. "Ah, don't be a prude Brick. I know you've endured fucking her to get more information on Were females, but it's the least you can do to put a show on for us one last time."

"No," Brick says, low and angry. I can't see his face anymore as Kilo and him are about to exit.

I should charge them and fight out of this cell, but Brick is a much better spy than I am because he succeeded. He broke me. I crumble to the floor, any ounce of my power, my feminine rage, squashed.

17

PIG ON THE RUN

I'm unsure how long my sorrow holds me, confining me to my cot in a tidal wave of tears. It's embarrassing. I don't see cameras hiding anywhere, but it would be a shitty prison if they weren't watching me. This isn't me. I don't crumble from rejection. Maybe it's the exhaustion and the pressing weight of my failure, but it feels much more helpless, as if I lost something precious. After what I assume is two nights, based on the timing of meals delivered to my room from the guards, I've tired myself of my wallowing. I must devise a plan to escape, even if it's futile.

I wait until I don't hear anyone outside of my door before transforming my claws and wedging a long, pointed tip into the space where the door and frame meet. I grow my nails longer, attempting to unlatch something. It's a stupid plan. Why would they lock me in a room so easy to escape? Kilo's a Were, at least half-Were. He should know our capabilities. But when something clicks and the door pushes toward me slightly, I nearly shit my pants. I did it. I unlocked the door.

I peer through a crack. No one stands guard on the other side. Could this be a trap, or do they really think I'm so incapable that they'd leave me unguarded? Probably the latter. They don't think highly of me, and I have been lying in bed crying for the past two days like a heartbroken teenage girl.

I don't contemplate. If this is a fuck up, it won't be long before someone realizes their mistake and captures me again. I attempt to shift before sprinting down the hall. Part of me follows my mental demands, but I can't change completely. Fuck. They must be drugging my food.

I keep my claws bared as I run down the hallway, crouching before every corner and attempting to stay near the walls. I have no sense of direction. There are no signs, no indication of where I should go, but I must flee somewhere, even if I'm running to an even worse fate. Some of my instincts must remain intact because I sense them—the other Weres. As I turn down a series of halls, my nose driving me toward their smell, I hope I'm being led to the captured girls and not a room full of traitor Weres like Kilo.

I turn sharply, coming to a locked room. A glass wall separates it from the hall, allowing a view into the room but with no access. Lara, Summer, and Victoria lie in separate small, glass cages–trapped like animals. They're in their human forms, wearing matching grey sets, the same as me. Their heads lull back and forth in their sleep, either from nightmares or the effects of drugs. They don't look injured, though. The only positive light to seeing them like this. I want to bang on the window and tell them I'm here, but that would be stupid. I can't rescue them now with my powers muted. I must find a way out of here and bring back the pack to rescue them.

It pains me as I turn away, running toward a hallway that somehow *feels* like the way out. I pass more rooms, wanting to stop and examine their contents through the glass. They appear to be testing rooms filled with vials, metal tables, and instruments that make my skin crawl just imagining their purpose.

I catch a door at the end of a long hallway. Something tells me it's the way out. I don't even take a complete step before someone grabs me from behind. I scream, but their large hand covers my mouth, blocking the noise. I kick against the mass of muscle, but it's futile. Whoever has me is much stronger, especially now with only half of my powers.

I expect a slew of darkly dressed guards to appear and Kilo to emerge behind them, cackling like the rat he is, but no one else is nearby. My attacker backs up, not letting their grip on me lighten until they open a door and shut us both inside, turning me toward their chest. It's dark, and my eyes grow wide, searching for any indication of my surroundings. I'm blinded when the attacker pulls a string, and light shines from a hanging lightbulb above. Brick stares down at me, his gaze hard and gray as he assesses me.

I'm stunned for only a moment before I pound against his chest, tears welling in the corner of my eyes. "You pig! I fucking hate you!" He covers my mouth again, his arm tightening on my lower back to still me.

He shushes me. "I just saved your ass."

I still, eyes wide. He removes his hand from my mouth, not letting it leave my chin. "What?" I ask in a whisper.

"You were about to walk into a room full of Hunters."

"Oh." Maybe my instincts are all out of whack. They tried to tell me Brick wasn't part of this, so they're obviously fucked up, which reminds me. "Why don't you want me to walk into a room full of Hunters?"

His face scrunches in disbelief. "Come on, Carmen. I didn't mean for you to get tangled up in this."

I push him back, unable to stand another second of him so close. "Why should I trust a word you say? You were lying to me all this time!"

"Oh, and you weren't? I knew you were only pretending to like me to get information from me."

Good. He should think I felt nothing. Maybe I can maintain a string of my dignity. "Obviously, you were playing the same game, just on completely different teams," I say, crossing my arms.

"Come on." He shakes his head. "You're smarter than that."

"Clearly you don't believe I hold any intelligence. You're a traitor, just like Kilo. You hate me as much as you hate what you are."

He steps forward, wrapping his hand around my neck. "Don't just think with your head, Carmen." He places his palm on my chest, over my heart. "There's something between us. Maybe we both started out trying to trick the other, but it changed." His lips rest inches from my own.

I shake my head, even as my breath heavies. "No, I was tasked to trick you to help protect our girls. You wanted to trick me to get more locations. Don't pretend we're the same."

"I'm not. We're so different—more than you know. But you must know that the Weres' safety is my highest concern. I've been working undercover for the National Department of Supernatural since I moved here three years ago. They wanted me to infiltrate true leaders like Kilo and needed concrete evidence. Something like this serum. Something to potentially counteract their attacks." He shakes his head, pain etching the lines of his features. "You infuriated me because you knew something was off with me right away. You know how many times you almost blew my cover? And then you fucked around with other cops right under my nose. I could fucking smell them on you." His grip tightens around my palms. "I could have set the world on fire. I had to stay away from you."

I attempt to move back but just squirm, searching his eyes for the missing piece. "What are you talking about?"

The words rush out of him as if he's been waiting for years to explain. "The Hunters summoned Kilo here to test out his blood serum. Kilo's pack spread fake information about defeating Hunters through back sources, and your pack picked up the bait. Kilo tasked me to trick you for a reason. I didn't know enough about their operation and the Weres were onto me. The Hunters trust me, but they keep me at an arm's distance. I've never even seen this facility until you were captured. Once I found out, I did everything I could for them to show me where you were. I said I'd been tired of being outside and would give up more locations of Were women if they let me in on the serum and the testing facility."

Damn. Well okay. That could explain everything. I shake my head. "No! How can I believe a word you're saying?"

He sighs, stepping closer, pinning me against a utility shelf. "Why would I lie to you now? What more could I possibly need from you? How do you think you got out of your room?"

"What? I picked the lock!"

He shakes and lowers his head. "I unlocked it. I bugged the system so the cameras showed an image of you lying in bed. I have the real feed on my phone. There are cameras everywhere, but I'm on watch tonight. But this place is still riddled with Hunters. This hallway is the only dark spot."

Okay, annoying. I had hoped I was somewhat capable of rescuing myself.

Brick's confession rushes over me, and I tense. If what he says is true, he's not off the hook, not even close. "Brick, you gave up locations. Weres are dead because of you." Hot tears form at the corner of my eyes.

He flinches as if I punched him in the gut. "I know, but I had to, or they'd never let me in." His voice cracks. "I did everything I could to protect them, to be there first on the scene so it wouldn't end ugly, but I failed. I want to protect Weres, but I've just caused hurt."

My anger turns to sympathy. I don't agree with his methods, but it's clear he's regretful. He looks so broken, so defeated. I place my hands on his chest and he rests his large palms over them. He blows out a breath as if my touch is all the reprieve he needs. But then his eyes change to a sharp focus. "I'm getting you out of here." He presses in closer, his eyes growing more intense by the minute.

The room is hot, his breath warming my face. I'm losing my fight, falling into the web I always find myself tangled in his presence. "Won't you blow your cover?"

"I'd blow everything for you." He grabs the back of my neck, bringing his lips to mine. My brain is liquid. I can't even contemplate the intensity of his words. There's no reason he should care for me so much—risk his life's work for me. But I don't care. My body sings a tune only for him, wanting nothing more than for him to strum my every cord. I open for him, allowing his tongue to stroke the inside of my mouth. I reach for his chest, attempting to pull the fabric away, wanting his flesh against mine. He must have the same idea because he pulls at the hem of my shirt, attempting to yank it off.

If I were in my right mind, I'd stop, ask more questions, and attempt to flee like Brick planned, but whenever I'm in his presence, I can't think straight. His fingertips leave burns in their wake as they run up my abdomen, branding me. I don't think anyone could touch me again with the same intensity. He paws at my breast, groaning into my mouth as he rocks his body against mine.

I reach for him, needing to feel the heat of his cock in my hand. God, is it glorious under my fingertips, long and thick, and the knot at the base sends another wave of anticipation through my core.

He brings his lips away from mine, dragging them to my ear. "Carmen, my little wolf."

I stroke him, reveling as he grows longer and harder for me. Minutes ago, I thought I'd never experience the feel of him again. Tears prick at my eyes. I didn't realize how much I'd miss this. I'd only had him a handful of times, but God, did it fill me with something foreign and savage. I need this man. I need him inside of me, coating me and making me his.

Brick pushes me back, his body turning rigid. I search his hardened expression. His ears have elongated, and they twitch overhead. "Someone's coming," he whispers. I can hear it now, footsteps growing closer. He straightens, shoving himself back in his pants and adjusting my clothing. "I'm sorry," he whispers, throwing me over his shoulder. "Scream," he orders. It's not hard to follow. I'm genuinely scared. I yell, pounding on his back.

"Good girl," he whispers before opening the door and stepping out into the blinding light of the hallway. "Got her," he says as he swings me to the ground and pulls my arms behind my back. I trust him now. Not just because of his words murmured in our close quarters, but because I felt the truth radiating from him. He cares for me in the same confusing way I care for him.

I play into the act, rearing back and snapping as if I meant to bite his flesh. "Fuck you!" I growl before glaring at Kilo standing before me.

"I saw her escape her room and try to hide in the closet." Brick reports to Kilo. It should scare me how good he is at putting on a show. Maybe I'll regret it later, but I know deep in my bones he isn't doing that with me.

I throw myself forward, attempting to escape from his grasp, but he holds me tightly, surely causing my wrists to bruise. Kilo taps his lip, examining me. My heart beats, scared he's catching on to our act. He circles around us, and I continue to struggle against Brick, waiting for Kilo's reaction.

Kilo places a hand on Brick's shoulder. "Good, man. I was worried you'd gone soft on me with this one, but this just proves your loyalty."

Brick grunts. "I'll take her back to her cell." He pushes me forward.

"Brick," Kilo calls from behind us. "We have special guests coming tomorrow—Hunters from my homeland. I'd like to put on a demonstration for them, specifically with the new discovery. Would you like to demonstrate on our little friend here? I know we can both smell that she's ripe for the picking."

Do I have my period and don't even know it? Jesus fucking Christ, this is weird.

"I'll do the demonstration," Brick says urgently. I don't know if I should be relieved or not that Brick will be there for whatever Kilo has planned, but as I sense his body tighten behind me, I know he's not looking forward to what's to come.

Brick doesn't say anything on our trek back to my cell. He holds me tightly, squeezing my wrists as if to encourage me to continue my fight. I remember him mentioning the cameras everywhere. We're not safe to act like our true selves now. He opens the door to my cell, but before he throws me inside, he strokes a finger down the back of my arm, a silent reminder of his care. He doesn't know how much it means to me.

He pushes me forward, half standing outside the doorframe. "Be ready for tomorrow," he says, his eyes drilling into mine as if to pass a message, but I can't gather what he means. "I will protect you, okay?" he whispers. He's bugged the cameras in my room, but I know he can never be too careful. This small statement is a considerable risk.

I nod. He lingers longer, examining me before shutting the door. I'm alone again, this time with more clarity, but it doesn't fill me with ease. Something is happening tomorrow. Something that chills Brick to his core. I trust him at his word to take care of me, but it doesn't leave me any less unsettled.

18

TEST PIG

No matter how close together the instances, you never get used to waking in an unfamiliar place. Bright white light shines above, making it take several moments to register the space around me. Chattering, I can't make out buzzes in my ear. I attempt to rub the fog away from my eyes but can't move my arms. That wakes me the fuck up. I panic, struggling against the binds around my wrists and ankles.

A man leans over me, holding a syringe. "Calm down," he whispers. He wears a mask and goggles, but his voice gives him away. He pretends to prick me with the needle, pressing against the side of my arm.

Brick is here. I'll be okay.

My memories from last night fill the gaps in my understanding. Nothing unusual happened after Brick left. I'd been fed a meal of flavorless soup and went to bed. It must have been drugged, knocking me out so I could be easily transported.

I turn my head, thankful I can move. I'm in one of the rooms I ran by the day before. White walls lined with metal tables of surgical equipment surround me. A group of suited men stand on the other side of a glass wall directly parallel to where I'm lying. Kilo stands at the center of the group, grinning at me. Maybe it's the effects of the drug, or maybe it's my new ability to look at him with the understanding of his true perversion, but he's grotesque. Before, he seemed lean but muscular, handsome, and carefree. Now, he appears lanky and sinister. I guess it's true that beauty is in the eye of the beholder, and once you know the real person, their entire image can change.

I divert my attention to Brick on my other side, unbagging a new syringe. Even in the white lab coat, goggles, and mask, he's still devastatingly handsome.

I think, even if he did turn out to be evil, I might feel the same way about him. His beauty is untouched by morality. Thank God he's a good guy, or my mind and body would have a confusing time. At least, I hope he's one of the good ones. I believe him, truly, but the rational part of me realizes I'm tied to a metal bed, and he stands next to me, fidgeting with equipment that could only be used for ill use. He must have a plan. I feel it within my marrow. I can't panic now.

Kilo's voice buzzes from a hidden speaker. "Brick, it seems we're ready. Why don't you explain to our guests what will happen."

"Yes, one second," Brick replies, dropping a metal forceps. He bends down to retrieve it, whispering to me. "Stay calm."

I attempt to let his quiet words wash over me, to become the calm he speaks of, even as my body shakes with fear. I must remain still and compliant. He pretended to give me something, most likely a sedative. If I freak out, I'll give him away.

Brick clears his throat, pulling down his mask and straightening his shoulders. "Thank you for being here, gentlemen. Today we have a demonstration for you. As you know, Kilo and his team have developed a serum that can transfer werewolf powers through the means of female werewolf menstruation. But there has been a recent discovery."

A recent discovery? Maybe we should have spent less time making out in a storage closet and more time explaining the evolution of this fucked up situation. I keep still, even as I tremble internally.

Brick clenches his jaw and his fists. "Today, we have a powerful female werewolf. Sedatives have stunted her powers, but we are still able to access her abilities even though she isn't menstruating."

The men whisper to each other on the other side of the glass, and Kilo's smile widens.

Brick carries on. "Although female Weres mentally control their cervix, allowing them to dictate when they want to become pregnant, they still experience a normal cycle every month."

Damn, why does he know more about my reproduction organs than me?

"The subject is currently ovulating."

What the fuck. How does he even know this?

He sniffs, holding in a groan as he presents a glass vial filled with a strange, almost glowing liquid. "I will be extracting her blood. Doctor Harold will combine the solution with this serum before injecting himself to demonstrate its effects." He motions to a man outside the room, framed by the viewing window. "This version of the serum isn't as powerful, but it leads to more opportunities to use the obtained werewolves to generate more defense."

So he's just going to take my blood so another creep can have a fraction of my powers? Okay, I guess this could have been a lot worse. Sure, we don't need more Hunters with our powers, but that's a problem for another day. Preferably when I'm not in captivity. From the way that I'm strapped to this table, it seems like they're going to harvest my organs. I relax a bit.

"I'll begin the extraction," I swear his voice quivers, and his hands shake as he picks up a needle on the small table, hovering over me. He gulps, his eyes heavy, before turning back to the onlookers. "Before the procedure, subjects are given an elixir that loosens their cells to release the power. We have found some primal reactions from subjects during these proceedings. I apologize in advance."

I raise an eyebrow at him, and he shakes his head, releasing a heavy gasp. His hand rests on mine, and our familiar electricity zips to life, but it's more like a lightning strike this time. My chest heavies. The moment he touches me, a switch flips inside of me. Does he mean that subjects get horny when they are having their blood drawn? God, they drugged me not only to dull my powers, but to make me aroused. I don't believe for a second it helps retrieve my power. From the shit-eating grin on Kilo's face, I suspect this is all for their sick enjoyment.

Thank God, Brick told me he had just been introduced to this place, or I'd be raging thinking about him arousing other Weres. That should be the least of my concerns because I have a inferno in my shorts. I writhe against my restraints, breathy moans leaving my lips. "Brick," I whisper like a prayer.

He grabs my arm, trying to steady me. It's the wrong thing to do. I cry out, my neck arching.

"Fuck," he whispers, turning away from me.

I'm on a metal table being watched by a group of men who want to see me dead, but all I can think about is Brick's skin against mine. I want him inside him—need him coating me with his cum. I've never been so aroused that it feels more like pain than plea-sure. The world washes away from me. The only focus in view is Brick's biceps, his large neck, and his hands running up my breasts. "Jesus Christ!" I yell. I work my legs together, needing an ounce of reprieve from the torture.

Brick turns back to me, exhaling through his nose. Determined to get this over with. He pierces my skin with the needle, pulling out my blood, but when his arm grazes against my skin, he whimpers. The sound nearly topples me over, but whatever they drugged me with isn't kind. My body will only sing if Brick is the one playing me. "Please, Brick. It hurts. Touch me."

His eyes water as he leans in, his mouth wide with a silent moan. He drops the needle to my side, his hand trailing down the center of me. I crane my neck, wanting his lips on mine. The veins in his neck bulge, and I watch as the skin toughens, mass making him bulkier. His nose and ears elongate slowly but enough to notice. It's not possible to be more turned on, but seeing him grow for me, contort into his animal form, makes pure pleasure seep from my pores.

My moans turn into a rhythmic pattern, as if instead of Brick trailing his finger from between my breast over my abdomen, my clothing still separating his touch, he is deep within me, wringing out the pleasure flooding my senses.

He lowers his lips to my ear. His breath heavy on my neck, his fingers trailing lower and lower until they reach the elastic band of my grey shorts. "Fuck me! Dear God, please!"

Brick pauses his dissent as if my words reminded him that I was here and he wasn't alone in his tempting pleasure. He balls his fist, groaning against my neck in agony.

Kilo's voice vibrates over the speakers. "Don't worry, Sergeant. You're free to do with her as you please. It's all a part of the presentation."

My disgust swats away some of the haze, and my body stiffens, remembering myself and the crowd of Hunters watching me. I turn away from Brick, taking in the group of businessmen. Some have their hands resting over the bulge under their slacks, some palm the window separating us, but all hold the same hungry stare. I knew the Hunters were evil, wanting to end our existence for some fucked up generational rivalry, but this is another level I've never seen firsthand, maybe didn't even believe it was real. Of course, Hunters had impregnated Weres using drugs and torture. They did it for power but also for the thrill of overtaking us. They hate us, but they also dream of us—their disgust turning into a primal longing.

Even as my head clears, my body refuses my thoughts. It needs Brick. My fingers still reach for him even as my binds hold me in place.

Something washes over Brick. He straightens his spine, his body shaking. A sob breaks from me as his proximity leaves me, and he takes a heavy step back. "We're done," he gets out through gritted teeth. His features melt, returning to his normal state.

"Ah, come on, Brick. Just think of her as an object. Surely, she can't repulse you that much," Kilo says through the speaker.

"She does," he says, his eyes watering, his hands clenched at his sides as if he's trying to break his fists from his body. "Take her to her room. The extraction is done." He slams the vial on the table before retreating to the other side of the room; arms folded over his chest and eyes not leaving me.

I'm still not in my right mind, but the intensity fades when he steps farther away from me. Two white-coated men barge into the room. I yelp, scared that Brick's effect on me will replicate with these strangers. I exhale once they wheel me out of the demonstration room and down the hall. I don't feel anything. The haze is wholly gone. That's until I catch Brick trailing behind us, watching me intently but keeping his distance. He doesn't leave my sight until I enter my prison. Two guards replace the men transporting me, freeing me from my binds and walking me to my cot. I'm still woozy from the drugs. I turn around on my bed as the guard leaves, not missing Brick's intense gaze, peering at me before the large metal door shuts behind the guards.

His eyes ignite the fire. I'm probably being watched. I can only hope Brick bugged the system, but there's no holding back as my fingers reach my sopping wet core.

19

PIGLETS

The lights in my cell never turn off, but they dim to a low, warm glow when I expect the Hunters want me to sleep. I've already rubbed myself to completion numerous times, not able to erase the image of Brick's smokey eyes from my brain. I assume it's been several hours, and I think the drugs are lessening. I'm beginning to feel more like myself. As reality settles over me, I kind of wish they'd drug me again. I nearly vomit, thinking about myself so vulnerable as the Hunters watched me with hungry stares.

I'm ready for sleep to take me into its darkness and end the horrible images from my mind, but my door creaks open. My heart hammers, and I sit up. Part of me fears it's one of the evil men wanting to take what they missed out on. A more significant part of me hopes it's Brick coming to save me. Or fuck me. Honestly, both would be nice.

I must be in some higher being's favor, because Brick slinks through the partially open doorway, glancing down the hall before peering at his phone in his hand. Well, I guess the higher being doesn't like me too much since I am trapped in some perverted torture prison, but I count my blessings when I can.

The moment his gaze meets mine, desperate and assessing, I realize the drugs haven't worn off at all. My weak attempts to satisfy my raging need were all for nothing because all I can focus on is my overwhelming arousal. I can't even work my legs to move toward him. My breath weighs me down as I attempt to hold myself up on my cot.

"Carmen, I'm so sorry," he says, taking small steps toward me.

"Brick, I need you."

He stops in his tracks. "No, Carmen. We have to get you out of here. I've been waiting to hear back from the National Department of Supernatural to get a team to get you all out. It's too risky to do it alone with the extra Hunters here, but they're taking too long. I've bugged all the cameras. Mostly everyone is out celebrating. I'm getting you out now."

His words register through my brain, but I can't focus on them. I gulp. "Brick, I don't know what they gave me, but if you don't fuck me this second, I feel like I might die."

He moves closer to me, his face more pained with every step. "They didn't give you anything."

This sobers me a bit. "What?"

"I switched the drugs. They give you a sedative every night. I knew if I switched that, they would be onto me, but I couldn't let them drug you with ecstasy. I couldn't let them take advantage of you like that."

My heart beats rapidly, and even though I'm trying to detangle Brick's words, I stick out my chest, my nipples hard and wanting. "Then what the fuck is going on? Why am I so horny?"

His look is sad as he reaches me, leaning over me and pinning me to lie back on the cot. "Carmen."

"What?" My hands wrap around his neck, attempting to pull his lips to mine, but he resists. His eyes pass a message to me, and I try to decipher his meaning.

"We're mates."

"No," but even as I say it, I arch my neck, pressing my lips toward him. His resisting ends, and he opens for me, pushing me down against the cot and grinding against me. He pulls away, but I hold on, kissing down his neck, his skin turning rough. "I knew it from the first moment I met you. My kind is more in-tuned to the mating bond," he says.

"I don't care." I groan, attempting to reach for his cock under his slacks. Reason or rationale is a foreign entity to me right now.

"I'm sorry, Carmen. I'm so sorry," he says, exposing more of his neck for me to lick. I work at unbuttoning him, and he shimmies out of his pants, holding himself up with one arm. I watch as his cock pops free from his briefs, and I gasp. It had been large last time, but now, it's even more so, thick and juicy and drops of cum dripping from the tip. "I'm sorry, Carmen. You're at the peak of your ovulation. I can't help it."

"Brick, goddamn." I reach for him, wrapping my fingers around his length, stroking him the best I can, even if it's a feeble attempt. He works himself out of his pants and briefs completely. When my gaze meets his again, I gasp. I've witnessed him on the brink of change before, but he always stops himself. His eyes are the same, but that's it. I've fucked a Were in their wolf form before, but Brick is not in a wolf form. He's not a werewolf. His ears were wide and flopping from the side of his head. Coarse hair covers all of him except his moist, flat snout. Two short horns crown his head. All this time, I've called him a pig because he was a cop, but he really is one.

I've heard of all types of variations of Weres, werepigs included. They're rare, dangerous, and primal. At least that's what I've heard. I've never witnessed one. Except now he's looming over me, cock thrusting in and out of my hand as he works to free my breasts from my thin cotton shirt. And this werepig—impossibly huge and ravenous, isn't just any werepig No, he's my mate.

"Do I repulse you?" he asks, a sadness in his voice.

I shake my head, honestly annoyed by the interruption. "No, now please, fuck me," I beg. I have so much to say to him, question why he didn't tell me the truth about so many things, and most importantly, to get the fuck out of here, but my body won't allow for anything else but being completely stretched by the fearsome boar before me. Goddamn, my fucking ovaries. Too bad I'm not letting them get their way completely. No piglets for me anytime soon.

I release his cock, wiggling out of my shorts from underneath him. He pulls my shirt overhead, holding me up in his arm to help. I can't kiss him on the lips anymore. His piggy snout is in the way, but it doesn't matter anyway as his wet and warm nose trails down my now bare body, swinging my legs over his shoulder once he meets my end. "God, I need to taste you. I need you on my tongue," he says, low and gruff, before holding my ass up and bringing his face to my burning core.

Even in my delirious mating frenzy, I can't deny that the thought of his snout digging its way into my cunt unnerves me, but I don't let the feeling take hold. Brick is my mate, destined as my perfect match. Whatever he has in store for me will be better than anything I've ever experienced.

His tongue meets my seam, long and thick and eager. He laps at me, and I feel myself flooding his mouth. I grab his horns, steadying myself as he licks me, long and languid. A wave of satisfaction runs through me at how perfect his handles are for riding his face. I've been eaten out before, but nothing has ever compared to this. His tongue is so wide and bumpy as he runs it over my opening. His wet nose hits my clit as he drives his tongue inside of me, and I cry out, the size of it honestly stretching me.

I bite my fist. Brick said he bugged the cameras so I can hope we aren't being watched, but I still know not to scream. It's a surprisingly rational thought, since nothing could stop me from reaching my edge. Not even if a militia of Hunters barged through the door. I'd ignore them entirely and complete my piggy ride.

My body clenches around his tongue, and my insides melt into a mixture of nothingness. My mind erases, only pleasure. Brick whimpers from underneath me, licking me more rapidly as if my rush of liquids is his sustenance. The satisfaction only lasts a moment. I yank on his horns, urging him up my body. The mating frenzy won't be sated. The only way to end our madness is to be filled and knotted; even then, it won't last long. I must be stuffed, and then we need to get the fuck out of here so he can pork me some more.

He crawls over me, his body at least doubled in size, his shirt ripped open. I suspect he's not fully in his pig form, although I have no idea what that looks like. When werewolves shift completely, it's almost impossible to decipher us from a wolf, except for our size and glowing eyes. Brick isn't a complete pig. I don't even know how that would work, so thank God. His face changed, all except his eyes, but his body is just large, covered with thick patches of hair over his chest, arms, and calves.

Of course, I want him desperately because of the hormones running through my body, but I can't help but marvel at his beauty. Maybe it's just my mind playing tricks on me. He's my mate, after all. I'm designed to want him, but he's just so fearsome, heavy breaths blowing from his snout. He's fucking hot.

He buries himself in the crook of my shoulder, positioning his cock at my entrance. "Carmen, I can stop. Say the word," he says against my neck, his breath labored and pained.

"Don't stop," I cry.

He inserts himself, not holding back. I bite into his skin to stop my scream, and my body clamps around the pain. He gives shallow thrusts, making room as he works deeper and deeper. I make way for him, pleasure blooming from the edges, turning into something delirious and delectable. He fucks me—hard and fast and without reserve. He reaches his hilt, the semi-deflated knot pushing its way in. A tinge of pain shoots through my body as it enters me, but it's quickly replaced by euphoria. My body was made for him, after all.

"God, Carmen, you fit me so fucking good," he says between thrusts. "This cunt is mine. Mine. Mine. Mine." He drones on, his words a wild plea. We're reaching our crescendo, our bodies stiffening, and our breaths increase in tempo.

My fangs burst through, and I clamp down on Brick's shoulder, tasting the metallic tang of blood. He ruts over the edge, slamming home and bursting inside of me. He fills me, seeping out and wetting my ass, but his knot grows, capturing his seed inside of me, filling me so completely I can almost taste him. My second orgasm rolls over me, long and lasting this time. I swim in it, letting it fill every broken piece of me.

Our bodies still, and silence settles over us. For the first time since Brick entered my cell, my mind clears. "Fuck," I mutter.

Brick looms over me, his features fading back to his usual self. "Fuck." He stares deep into my eyes.

Now we're stuck like this.

Brick's eyes dart over my face, working on untangling something or examining if I'm okay, maybe a bit of both. "This was a mistake."

Obviously, but I can't help the sting. He must notice the shift in my expression. He grabs my chin. "No, you're not a mistake. God, Carmen. I want nothing more than to fuck you for the rest of my days. But, this." He motions down to where our bodies still connect. "This is a mistake. I was supposed to get you out of here." He looked like he might cry, completely defeated.

I run my fingers through his hair. "Hey, it's okay." It's not. "We're still getting out of here. What's another twenty minutes?"

He scrunches his face. "Twenty minutes? It won't take that long?"

"Really?"

"Carmen, this isn't our first time."

"Yes, but I guess I wasn't paying attention. There wasn't a rush last time."

"Is that how long werewolves take?" He smiles incredulously.

I shrug. "I mean, yeah, I guess."

He scoffs. "It won't be that long. Maybe like ten."

"Hm, I didn't realize pigs didn't last long." I smirk.

"Hey, I can last long. My sperm is just efficient. It doesn't need twenty minutes to reach the finish line."

I shrug. "Well, it can be as fast as it wants. It's not entering that winner's circle."

His cocky expression shift. "No, of course. I would never knot you if I didn't know you'd have control over your body."

I raise an eyebrow. "Really?"

"Carmen! What kind of man do you think I am?"

I shrug. "I'm just kind of disappointed."

"Shut the fuck up." He sighs.

I tsk. "I'm just saying, you know, considering that I actually want it, it would be kind of hot if you just couldn't control yourself around me." Maybe it's the depravity of my situation. Maybe it's my mind's sick way to make humor out of a traumatic situation, but I find myself fucking hilarious. I can't help making him squirm.

"Carmen, you're imprisoned right now, and instead of breaking you free as I planned, I'm stuck inside of you. I think it's pretty clear that I can't control myself around you."

I consider and shrug. "Touché."

He exhales, falling into the crook of my shoulder. "God, are you frustrating."

"Is your cock getting hard?" I wiggle underneath him, feeling his knot deflating and his dick pressing against the walls of my pussy.

He smiles, his teeth pressing against my neck. "Maybe I like your attitude more than I should."

"That's one way to get us unstuck."

He pulls himself free of me, but his lips remain on my neck. His new wave of arousal washes over me with sticky strokes. But he straightens, sitting up and retrieving his clothes.

I sit up, searching for my grey prison uniform. "So... you're a pig. Like for real."

He eyes me, stepping into the leg of his pants. "I'm a werepig, yes."

I nod. It's silent as he buckles his pants, examining his ripped shirt before pulling it over his shoulders, hanging open thanks to the missing buttons. "Does that bother you?"

I shake my head, reaching for him. "No." He sits next to me, taking my hand in his. "Just why didn't you tell me?"

He sighs. "I knew we were mates the minute I saw you. I tried to fight it, tried to keep my distance but life kept throwing us back together. I learned everything I could about you."

"Is that how you knew where I lived?

"What?" His eyes grow, guilt-ridden.

"When you were drunk, you told me when and how much I bought my house for."

He drags a hand down his face. "God, I'm an idiot. I can't apologize enough for that night. I think it was the alcohol and the mating bond that made a mess of my brain. I was all over the place." He shakes his head, his cheeks red. It's kind of adorable. He sighs. "Maybe I did some light stalking, but I had to learn more about you."

I scrunch my lips. "Light, huh?"

He waves his hand. "That's beside the point. What I'm trying to say is, I never thought I'd find a mate. There aren't many werepigs, and I didn't think it was possible to mate with a different species of Weres. But when you burst into my office, raging and accusing me of fucking up my job on purpose, I was so angry. I knew what you were right away; your family's history was in my files, and it infuriated me."

"Wanted a pig-lady?"

"No, it's not that." He pulls me closer, positioning me on his lap. "I didn't think you'd want me. You are so beautiful and strong. I'm a hideous beast. I was able to control shifting before, but with you at the height of your ovulation, I couldn't hold back."

"I'm glad you didn't hold back. I think you're pretty fucking hot."

He smiles, tucking a strand of hair behind my ear. His eyes grow somber. "That's not the only reason I tried to keep you away. I was sent here to infiltrate the Hunters, working as a triple agent. I didn't want to bring my mate into this mess. And yet..." He looks around the room, his body growing rigid as he stands, pulling me with him. "Come on, we got to get out of here." The world comes back to view. This is hardly the time to be fucking and sharing our life stories. Our mating frenzy still clearly clouds our judgment, making it hard to think about anything else but each other, even escaping.

As if on cue, steps bring our attention to the opening doorway. Kilo walks through, clapping slowly. My body tenses, and my stomach rolls. Is he fucking serious?

"What a little performance you put on there! I would have come in earlier, but I thought it would be rude to barge in while you two detangled yourselves."

Brick's arms tense, and he grows, his pants tightening, and his shirt pulls away from his bare chest. "I wouldn't get all piggy on me, Brick." A swarm of guards barge into the room. I'm still under the effects of drugs. If I had my full powers, I could help Brick fight these mortals off, except their eyes are glowing. They're using the serum composed of werewolf blood.

Brick must notice as well because he doesn't attack.

Kilo clasps his hands behind his back, rocking on his feet. "I still wouldn't doubt you if you came in to fuck her, but then you had to share your whole sob story." He shakes his head. "I'm not an idiot, Brick.

I didn't trust you from the beginning. When Grimm suggested Carmen pretend to like you to get information, I tried to steer them away, but then I thought: why not? I had my instincts about you." He taps his nose. "One of the benefits of being a Were. I decided to throw you in to see where your loyalty lies. I figured, allowing the Weres to couple you two together would be the perfect test to my theory. Capturing her, bringing you here to watch you." He shakes his head. "Do you really think I'd give you so much trust—allowing you to be the only one on guard, giving you access to security—when we only just recently decided to allow access to our facility? I don't know how you made it this far in your police career, honestly. You're so easy to read. For your sake, I hope it's just the effects of the mating bond, dumbing you and making you sloppy." He smiles, and Brick lunges for him, shifting in an instant.

I was right when I suspected he wasn't entirely in his pig form earlier. He isn't a pig who walks on four feet, though. He's bipedal, thunderously large, with hooves replacing his feet. I guess that could explain the hoof prints at the crime scenes. His hands are still humanoid but clawed and covered with thick hair. I can't look away. Mesmerized by his strange and savage beauty.

Brick almost reaches Kilo, but the guards zoom to meet him. Five surround him, faster than humanly possible, and bring him to the ground. "No!" I yell, not noticing the two guards cornering me, one of them pricking me with a syringe. I struggle against their grip, but it's no use. My vision tunnels. The last thing I see before everything goes black is Brick pinned down by five guards, clearly drugged with werewolf strength, but struggling still as my werepig thrashes. He watches me, accepting defeat—the same smokey eyes I know so well, riddled with panic.

20

BLOODY PIG

Coming back to consciousness again feels like an overdone plot point. There must be some serious side effects to being put out so frequently. Still, as I take in my surroundings, the sterile laboratory from before, I realize I have far more significant problems to worry about. I'm strapped to a metal table again. It's boring, honestly, but this time, I'm not the only victim imprisoned. Brick is in a chair beside me, his head lulled to the side, his hands behind his back. His chest rises and falls, letting me know he's drugged and still alive. I sigh in relief, but it's short-lived. I turn my attention to the man standing at my other side; Kilo is visibly giddy that I'm awake.

"Good morning. You're just in time for some fun. I love it when they're conscious."

I groan. "Kilo, do you have to be so stereotypical?"

He ignores my pleas, picking up a manila folder at the small table to my side. "You know, I envy you, truly." I don't reply, because clearly, he's having this conversation with himself. "You think you deserve a full life. You're not disgusted with who you are. What I would give to live as blind as you." His words shouldn't affect me, but I can't help feeling sorry for him, as fucked up as it sounds. I can't imagine the world he was reared in, filled with torture, teachings of self-loathing, and lack of love. He's entirely in control of his actions. Everyone can choose between good or evil, and I hope that if I were raised in the same environment, I might make the right decision. I'll never know for sure, and although my upbringing wasn't easy, I'm thankful that it didn't lead me to this moral crossroad. It's my job to ensure people like him cease to exist and create a better world for future generations. It's not just my noble cause, it should be everyone's.

"Kilo, it doesn't have to be this way. You are not inherently dirty. You can live a good life full of love." I try, but I know it's a feeble attempt. I imagine other women have dished out the exact same words. There's nothing special about me that could make the truth sink in. He's too far gone.

"That's cute," he says, patting my arm, his eye skimming back in his folder. "At first, I did enjoy this whole thing you've got going on. So sure of yourself, so confident. I was a little jealous of Brick for having all the fun." He leans in. "I could tell you two were mates. I decided to try to build a wedge between you. See if you could open those pretty legs for me just like you did for everyone else in this shit-hole town."

I bare my teeth, unable to grow fangs and snap at him. He darts back, laughing, and I realize that's exactly what he wanted me to do.

Brick groans from beside me, chains jingling as he attempts to move his arms. It's surprising that we're tied up so close. If we could break free from our binds, we could touch each other. But once he opens his eyes and they settle on me, I realize the placement is not a kindness. Need washes over me, and I struggle against my binds. Brick closes his eyes and clenches his jaw, visibly in pain.

I've known my whole life that the mating bond was powerful, especially on a Blood Moon, but the Blood Moon isn't happening right now, and the tether between us is white hot, nothing like I've ever experienced or witnessed. Maybe it's because he's different, not a werewolf, but a werepig. Maybe their mating frenzy is more intense. It's the only logical conclusion.

"Ah, Brick! Just in time for the fun," Kilo cheers.

I should be freaking out. I'm helpless, and the other half of my heart is bound next to me, to witness my demise before succumbing to his own. But all I can focus on is the raging fire in my core. I've never thought pleasure could be such torture.

"Kilo, I'll fucking kill you," Brick seethes, turning his attention away from me.

"It doesn't look like that's going to happen." He walks around the table and stops at Brick's side, folder still in hand. "You know what I hate more than Weres? Weres who know the truth, who have been privy to the reality of our sickness and choose to procreate anyway. You're a special kind of perversion, a pig. We almost eradicated your kind, and yet you persevered. It would be noble for you to join our fight, but all you care about is fucking this dog, spreading your disease to new, disgusting heights."

Neither of us respond, whether out of the knowledge that it wouldn't matter or the will to focus on anything other than our throbbing sexes. Probably a mixture of both.

Kilo taps on his folder. "The mating rituals between you freaks have truly been fascinating. The ovulation period of a female makes things so much more exciting. I can't help but play with my experiments, especially during their heightened cycle and after giving them ecstasy. One thing I've missed in my studies is having two mates together at the same time. What would happen if I'm the one to ring the pleasure of your mate while you sit back and watch? What kind of power could I extract from both of you?"

Brick shifts fully, his face that of a wild boar, every inch of his body covered in thick brown hair. He roars, yanking against his chains that barely budge. Kilo squeals in delight. "Yes! This is exactly the kind of reaction I've hoped to see! I can't wait to document this." He waves the folder before walking to the other side of me and placing it on the table. "This is getting full with all my discoveries. I'll be using this to write a book soon. Then all the Hunters from all over the world will know how to harvest female Were menstruation for their power, and they can have a bit of fun with the ovulation bit, too. What's a life without pleasure? Wouldn't you two agree?"

"Brick," I cry. It's the wrong thing to do. The words slipping from my lips cause him to shudder, losing his focus on his anger. I need him mad. I need him to break free and rescue us both.

Kilo runs a finger from my foot up my body, traveling over the ridge of my breast covered by my gray prison uniform and stopping at my lips. "Don't worry. I'd never fuck a beast like you. But I can touch, explore. That's what science is, after all."

Brick roars from next to me, and I whip my attention to him. He's enormous, his arms squeezing in his tight bonds. The chair must be welded to the ground, because it doesn't budge. I don't think the drugs affect his powers at all. It must be silver. Werewolves grow powerless when bound with it. I guess werepigs are similar to us in that aspect. "Your sad attempts of male domination won't help you now,

Brick. I've sent everyone home so we can have all the fun to ourselves."

His words focus me through my lust-filled haze. It's only us and the prisoners. We just need to overtake one pathetic man and we can get out of here. It's an idiotic move on his part, but he must trust the effects of the drugs over me and the integrity of Bricks binds. If only I could grab a hold of my power from somewhere deep inside of me. I'm ovulating, apparently something that can give normal humans powers once harnessed. I just need to find the strength within myself and use it to escape. Sure, I'm strapped to a metal table, but I could break free if I used all my might—if I shifted.

Kilo's finger travels lower, and I can't help the breathy moan that passes my lips. I swear Brick's eyes turn red. I close my eyes as Kilo's touch moves between my breasts, rolling down my stomach. Instead of Kilo's fingers, I imagine Brick's, tuning in to his yelps of desperation, pretending they're that of need for me. I trick myself, imagining my stomach filled with Brick's baby. His hand rubbing my swollen belly, whispering soothing words to our soon-to-be child. It's not something I want, at least not right now. I barely know Brick, but my instincts as his mate takes over. It's not hard to imagine carrying his baby and starting a family with him. I can play pretend, at least for now. At least to trick my body into needing my mate so severely that it overpowers the chemicals swimming through my veins. It's a lofty hypothesis, but it's all I got.

Just as Kilo's fingers meet the hem of my shorts, something combusts inside me. All my nerve endings turn to fire, my blood lava—red washes over, a deep and desperate anger, blinding me of my senses. I feel the snap, I hear the screams, but it's as if they're a story being played from somewhere else, not from my actions. Consciousness rolls back to me in soft waves, more of my awareness returning to me like a windshield wiper clearing away the frost. My lungs heave in my chest. It's silent, and my heart pounds steadily. I'm seated on the metal table. My hands aren't human; they're monstrous claws, furry and dripping with blood. Noticing the carnage focuses me, and I remember myself, cradle my head, and feel my snout and muzzle.

"Carmen!" Brick yells, repeating himself in a desperate plea. I whip toward him, still bound, and in his werewpig form. "Brick?" I get out, my voice a foreign sound. "What happened?" The hairs on the back of my neck loosen, sucking back into my pores.

"Are you okay?" he asks desperately.

I contemplate myself, feeling no pain, returning to myself every moment. "Yes. What happened?"

"You shifted. You broke free and attacked Kilo."

I look down at the ground, taking in Kilo's blooded body. His eyes are wide, and he clutches his neck, a chunk removed and sputtering blood in a large pool underneath him. I'm back to my human self now, naked, my ripped clothes beside me, and covered in blood. I stand, stepping around Kilo, wobbling momentarily before catching my bearings. I kneel next to him, and he reaches for me, but I swat his hand away, diving into his deep lab coat pockets. I pull out a large ring of keys.

I charge toward Brick, my throat void of moisture as I approach, my bare chest pinched tight with arousal from the sight of him. "Carmen," he moans thoughtlessly as if a single-minded beast put on this earth to devour me. In fact, that's precisely what he is. I guess that's what I am, too, since I just killed a man to reach him, to have his knot inside of me.

My hands shake as I work through the keys, inserting one after another into the keyhole attached to the metal chains around Brick's wrists. Finally, one clicks, and the chains fall to the ground. Brick stands like an angry dark wave sucking the energy from the room. I'm nearly knocked off my feet, but his arms wrap around me, roaming my skin with desperate groans. "Brick," I try to form a reason to tell him no and that we need to go, but his touch is too demanding, too desperate. I can't form words, and I comply as he drags me to the metal table, his snout flicking over my neck. He turns and bends me forward, and I moan as his fingers search for my heat, pulsing as he touches my wetness.

His pants haven't ripped off him during his shift. They must be made of heavy-duty, stretchy material. He pulls his cock free, grunting and moaning as he positions himself at my entrance. I arch for him, grinding my ass against him in a hungry plea. I can't focus on anything but the warmth from his head as he pushes it inside of me. My cunt makes way for him, stretching easily.

He roars, thrusting in and out with so much power that if I hadn't regained some of my own, I'd surely be knocked off my feet. I cry out as he moves deeper within me, reaching his hilt and shoving in his half-deflated knot. "My mate. Mine," he growls in my ear. His voice isn't his own, a deep monster claiming him.

My nerves tighten and if I thought something combusted in me earlier, I was clearly mistaken. An atomic bomb destroys me as my orgasm bursts to its height, taking my vision, taking my sense of self. I'm a bundle of nerves, exploding into a dark, warm hole. I register Brick crying out from behind me, slapping against my bare ass until he bursts inside of me, filling me with his seed as his knot inflates within me, stretching me so deliciously that I come again, less intense this time but longer lasting.

It takes what feels like hours but is probably only seconds to come down, regain myself, and take hold of my breath. Brick falls on top of me, barely holding himself up, and my legs quiver, attempting to take his weight. I look down, witnessing the blood from underneath me, smeared from my body, and on the ground lies Kilo, his eyes blank and his body stilled. "Fuck," I mutter, pushing myself up. Brick jolts from behind me, removing his weight and grabbing me. He attempts to turn me to him, but we're stuck. "Fuck," he whispers, sad and defeated. I reach back, feeling his neck, running my hand against his chiseled jaw. He's already returning to his human self.

"I'm sorry, Carmen. It wasn't me."

"No, it's okay. I felt the same way. We're okay."

"Fuck, no. We're not okay. We need to get out of here."

I caress down his skin, pebbled with stubble, trying to calm his panic I sense rising. "If what Kilo said is true, we're the only ones here. It will be okay. This had to happen. We wouldn't have gotten far without knotting. Our bodies wouldn't allow it."

My words settle him, and he leans into me, sniffing my hair and roaming his hands over my stomach. "You did it. You saved us."

"I guess so."

"How did you shift?"

"I don't know. I think it was because I was ovulating. I willed myself to imagine being impregnated by you."

He tenses. "You did?"

I pat him. "Don't worry. Your sperm hasn't reached my eggs, and now that I'm thinking clearly, I'm building that wall."

He kisses the back of my neck. His cock hardens inside of me, his knot deflating. "God, thinking about you carrying my child does something to me. That must be the hottest fucking dirty talk I've ever heard."

I laugh, the sound so foreign in the cold, lifeless room. "You're a freak."

His teeth graze over my skin. "I'm your freak, forever."

Forever. The word hits me—the implications of having a mate. I haven't had time to register all of this, and now is not the time to do so. I straighten, and Brick falls from me with a pop, his semen running down my legs. "Fucking, Christ." He moans, stepping away from me, clenching every part of himself as if in an attempt to steady.

I'm a fucking mess, covered in blood and semen. My clothes ripped to shreds from my shift. A fresh lab coat hangs in the corner, and I grab it, pulling the fabric over myself.

Brick glances at me briefly but diverts his attention. "God, Carmen. A lab coat? Why?" He whimpers, rubbing his eyes as if the sight pains him, before shoving himself back in his pants.

"It's all I have. Please, Brick. Will yourself to focus." I can't imagine that I look appetizing at this moment, but to my mate, I'm apparently a Michelin star meal. He takes a deep breath, steadying himself.

My eyes catch the manila folder atop the metal table. I grab it, skimming the contents. "Jesus Christ." My stomach churns, but I force myself not to look away. There are pictures of werewomen, lying unconscious and bare. Notes are scribbled next to the images, describing what's happening, but I don't believe it for a second. This wasn't science for Kilo. This was a perverted way to get himself off. He hates Weres so much that he became obsessed, finding pleasure in our torture. I hold back my bile, my eyes landing on a detailed report of the serum. "Brick, look." I hand him the file, and his eyes scan, widening as he takes in the information. "This is it. This is what we've been looking for. This could give us what we need to counteract their attack, to find an antidote for their discovery."

Could it really be this easy? Kilo brought us into a room, alone with the answers so close. It's idiotic of him, but it makes sense. He was a sick man, driven to desperation that clouded his sense of reasoning. I can't waste time pondering his actions. We need to get the fuck out of here.

I grab my mate, folder in tow, and open the metal door. We have women to free, an evil establishment to dismantle, and all of this is just the beginning.

21

WILD BOAR

I stand atop a hill, the concrete square building below. Swarms of police and suited unknown men trail in and out of the structure, like a group of ants excavating a box of sugar. Except the contents inside are far less sweet, a cube of torture and depravity.

It's been mere hours since Brick and I exited the facility, both of us filthy, exhausted, and dragging out the three drugged women we rescued. It didn't take long for Cameron to pick up our scent through the woods. His shoulders deflated the moment he saw me, tears in his eyes as he cradled my jaw and pulled me in close. That's when I lost it, sobs rushing out of me. The last few days' events crashed over me in a wave of relief and exhaustion. I didn't let the hug last long, as I was still naked besides the lab coat held together by a rope I found, and covered in Kilo's blood and Brick's semen. Not a state to be in when embracing your brother.

After that, everything was a whirl. The pack came, the National Department of Supernatural was called, helicopters buzzed overhead, and I was taken to a nearby pack member's house to shower and given a clean set of clothes. My body moved from one task to the next, only focusing on my present actions instead of contemplating the recent events and my newfound mate.

Now, the tension has died. The girls are safe and in medical care, finally coming into their consciousness, I'm told. I catch Brick closer to the building, his expression clenched and his arms crossed. Someone must have loaned him their coat because his previously bare chest is covered with brown wool. His eyes catch mine, and his jaw loosens, his eyes blazing even from many feet away. My heart drums as he makes his way over to me, climbing up the steep hill as if it's nothing. Even with the crowd, my cells burst into song, begging me to run the rest of the way and meet him with an embrace. I steel myself, holding my breath until he's inches from me.

"What's going on?" I ask, willing my brain to focus on his response instead of my stupid fucking need.

"It's a shit show," he says under a heavy breath. "They're all gone. Everything is wiped."

"What? How?"

He sighs, rubbing down his face, standing next to me to take in the view of the said shit show before us. "We set off an alarm when we escaped. I turned it off before coming to get you, but you know, that was a while ago."

Recent memories of our heated moments together rush around me. I shiver, Brick's touch imprinted on my skin. "Honestly, I'm surprised we even made it out of there with the girls."

Brick nods. I feel his gaze on me even as I look ahead, searing into the side of my skull. "We're lucky. But you kicked ass."

I throw the thought around, watching it overhead. "Hm, I guess I did."

"And that file, even if we can't arrest anyone for their atrocities, we have the serum. The National Department of Supernatural will be all over this town now. That file is enough evidence to really put an end to this."

I let out a heavy sigh. It's good news, truly, but I've heard it all before, in a thousand different ways. The girls are free, and Kilo is dead, but there are a hundred other men just like him. When one gets chopped down, another bursts through the murky surface just as quickly. I should feel glad, proud of myself, but I just feel tired.

Brick grabs my elbow. Okay, maybe not just tired. My body vibrates.

He pulls me into his embrace, kissing the top of my head. I stiffen at first. We're out in the open, in the light of day, and he holds me as if I'm his. I fight my brain's instinct to reject the affection and instead lean into him, feeling a million times better once I surrender. Besides the whole buzzing vagina. God dammit I hate ovulation.

I catch Cameron's gaze from below. He studies me oddly, but then something like understanding covers his features, and he nods with a smile. I smile back, shaking my head as if this is all a major annoyance. He rolls his eyes and returns to his conversation with the police. The cop isn't anyone I'm familiar with. I surmise they're special officers flown in.

"You did good, little wolf," he kisses down the side of my face, his length pressing into my backside.

I giggle, stiffening to stop his travel. "Brick, we've already gone too far during enough inappropriate times."

"What's one more?" he says mid-kiss.

"We have a lot to discuss," I counter, flipping to face him and lacing my arms around his neck.

He scrunches his face. "I don't know if you know this about me, but I'm not a talker."

I laugh. "In fact, that is one of the very few things I know about you. That's what we need to talk about. You're my mate. There's still so much to figure out." "I know, but we have forever to do it." He kisses me gently. "But right now, you're in heat, and I'm a wild boar that can't control myself."

I almost surrender, turn my bones to liquid, and let him carry me down the hill and fuck me behind a tree, but we're interrupted. "Carmen, Brick!" Grimm calls from the base of the hill.

I groan but stuff away my desire, eager to hear from my pack's leader. Grimm hurries his steps, throwing his arms around me in a desperate hug. It's strange, and I stiffen. Grimm and I have never hugged before, but I relax into it after a moment. Maybe finding my mate is making me all fluffy.

He pulls back, examining me. "I can't tell you how sorry I am. I just can't believe you were captured moments after I was with you."

I shake my head. "It's fine." I honestly haven't even considered it. I was the one who hurried him to leave. Maybe if I had been honest and revealed more of my thoughts, I wouldn't have put myself in the situation. But then we wouldn't have gotten to the facility and broken the girls free.

"No, it's not fine." His pupils dilate. I take in his unkempt hair, an oddity for him, and the deep bags under his eyes. "I brought Kilo into our pack, put you in danger, and then doubted you."

"I agreed to all of it. I trusted Kilo, too." I attempt to erase the image of his lips on me, the thought sending my stomach into an upheave.

My words don't seem to soothe Grimm. "I should have vetted him better. I did my research but clearly it wasn't enough. Even Cameron suspected something funny with him. Not at first, but he caught on quickly. I just blamed it on his pregnancy hormones. I was blinded, desperate for someone to save us."

I grab his arm, attempting to steady his spiral. "Grimm, we all were desperate." I trusted him as well. Just because Grimm is our leader doesn't mean he's immune to mistakes.

He breathes out, studying me. "Turns out the one to save those girls was right under our noses. You did it, Carmen. I shouldn't have doubted you."

"Well, maybe you should have." I motioned my eyes toward Brick, and Grimm takes him in as if forgetting he was there.

"Brick, I apologize for not trusting you, but I've got to say, you could have just told us you were working as a double agent."

Brick shakes his head. "It was too dangerous for any of you to know. Also, if you knew, Kilo would have known, too. Although I've learned he had his suspicions."

His guilt-ridden expression comes back in full gleam. "Fucking hell. You're right." He yanks at his hair.

Brick slaps a hand on his shoulder. "When's the last time you slept?" Clearly noticing the exhaustion.

Grimm groans, pulling his phone out of his pocket and glancing at the screen as he replies. "What I need is a goddamn secretary."

A loud crash sounds from behind us. We turn toward the road below, at the base of the hill, opposite the laboratory. Someone crashed into the shiny red Porsche parked on the side of the road, right around the bend.

"You have to be fucking kidding me!" Grimm yells, leaving us and racing down the hill.

"Was that his car?" Brick asks, moving in close.

"Yep." I wince, watching as a young woman with blonde-almost white-long hair emerges from the beat-up brown Volkswagen, now smashed against Grimm's sports car.

"Hey, it's a pretty girl. Maybe he'll go easy on her." Grimm reaches the offender at the end of my statement, and I can practically see the steam leaving his ears as his yells travel to my eardrums. I sigh, shaking my head. "Just what he needs."

My attention diverts as two strong arms wrap around me and pull me against a wall of muscle. "It's just what I need. Now I have you alone."

I motion to the swarm of people below. "We're not really alone."

He rolls his eyes and swats in their direction. "Forget about them. Whenever I'm with you, it feels like it's just the two of us."

My heart swells at his words, and I kiss his lips, allowing the affection to linger as his hands feel my back. He pulls back. "Although, I much rather actually be alone with you."

I sigh with a grin. "Fine, ravish me." I fall into him, removing my effort to hold myself up. He doesn't hesitate, swinging me over my shoulder as I squeal and hit his back. He jogs, bouncing me along until we're hidden behind a dense forest. He shifts, raising me slightly as his body grows in height and mass. He's still clothed, an attribute I envy, but his speed increases as he charges through the woods, carrying me to God knows where. I could ask, but I don't bother. Where my mate goes, I'll follow. Technically right now, I'm swung over his shoulder without any say in the matter, but I know our destination ends with me being fucked silly, and who am I to complain about that?

22

HOUSE OF BRICK

I'm out of breath, huffing and puffing on my knees. I dig my nails into the sculpted thighs, sandwiching me into the tight space. He's so large, filling my mouth entirely. I use my hand to lather the remainder of him, working my damned hardest to make this pig lose himself, and sputter deep into my throat.

I glance up at him, his eyes clenched and his fingers working through my hair, doing everything to steel himself—to model his signature bricklike persona. I shut my eyes. It's too much for me to look at him, lost in the pleasure of my lips. I always lose. He'll have me coming several times before knotting me. No matter how hard I blow this house of brick, he never crumbles—insisting his seed fills me where his instincts demand.

He groans, and his body tightens. I bare down, using all my werewolf strength to pin myself in place, but I'm no use. He grabs my hair, yanking me back, and his cock falls out of my mouth with a pop, a string of saliva connecting my lips to his tip. We freeze, waiting for our next move.

He's transformed. I stare into his smokey eyes above his flat snout, breathing long and heavy breaths. Seeing him in his werepig form always does something to me. More than normal, which is saying a hell of a lot since I can't get my hands or cunt off of this man, even now that my ovulation is over with.

I bite my lip, the tension thick between us and becoming too much. The small movement does it for him, and in one swoop, he catches me in his arm, carrying me the short distance to his bed and dropping me atop the white comforter. I squeal in delight as he folds over me, nuzzling his wet nose into the crook of my neck.

"You never let me have my fun," I whine through labored gasps.

"You sound like you're having fun." His fingers trail down my body, seeking out the heat between my legs. "You feel like you're having fun."

I moan as he teases my seam, so delicate that I press against him for more. That's me, always wanting more, and he continues to make me wait and beg for it. I'd throw a fit, but God, do I love it. I love everything about this man. In fact, so much so that as he dives his fingers in deeper, thrusting into my entrance and rubbing my bud simultaneously, I can't help by saying, "God, I love you."

He shivers, his teasing touch gone and replaced with determination as he whispers into my ear. "I love you more, little wolf." It's not the first time we've said it to each other, not even close. It's been about two weeks since he carried me off the hill, overlooking the block of doom. Two weeks without leaving each other's sides besides the ever-annoying work. I'm able to work from home, but Brick has had to leave every day, suiting up in his tan lieutenant garb, leaving me for hours, sitting in my desperate want for him.

Thankfully, I had loads of work to keep me busy. I'm still not allowed to finish my exposé on the Hunters. The Federal Department of Supernatural forbids me from revealing their—but really my—bust so other Hunters don't go into hiding. I've moped about it, but I found some good use of my time. Specifically researching every illegal and shitty thing Officer Wood has ever done and blasting him in his own exposé article. I also told Brick about him trying to sexually assault me. Maybe not the best idea since he left in a fit of rage and returned hours later covered in suspicious amounts of blood, but I don't stick my nose where it doesn't belong. Okay, maybe I do, but this seemed like something that would be better if I kept my deniability. Besides, Wood deserved every horrible thing that came to him. It's about time some evil pigs got blown the fuck down.

I'd thought that when my ovulation was over with, I'd be able to think more rationally. A part of me feared that once my wits returned, I'd go back to loathing Brick, but the opposite happened. After the sticky, suffocating heat washed away, all that was left was the kernels of reasoning for our predestined pairing. I still can't get enough of him, and although we still bother each other with our sometimes polar opposite personalities, it makes everything so much more fun.

Of course, I love this man. It's more than a mating bond. He's everything to me. Crazy how something so soul-catching could manifest in such a short amount of time.

"Dear God!" I yell, the pleasure closing in on me, firing up my nerves into a roaring flame. "That's it, baby. Worship me with your cunt." Brick rings out every last drop from me, before removing his hand and replacing his length, barely giving me a moment before rutting inside of me. Three shallow thrusts and he's completely inside of me, his semi-inflating knot stretching my entrance, sending something fierce through my nervous system.

"I'm so close." His breath is hot on my skin, and he's unable to hold himself back as he pounds his way home. "So tight, so perfect," he murmurs more encouraging phrases, lost in a ramble of pleasure. He tightens again, winding me up, and we both crash at the same time—the climb reaching its max. We fall together into a warm spring, swimming until we wash up on the shore, lying in silence. He inflates, stretching me further. It has its pain, but I revel in it, digging my nails into his now-human back.

He smooths my hair, peppering kisses at the side of my face. "God, I love you."

I smile. "You're just saying that because you're stuck with me. Literally."

He shakes my head. I'm only teasing, and he knows it, but I'm eager to hear his witty retort. I love his mind, the way he never lets my mouth run without catching my baton. He sighs and I think maybe he's too sated to play our game, but then he parts his lips, his voice velvet and cracked pepper. "Before I met you, I didn't believe in divinity. I'd been alone in this world, *other than* to every being around me. I only had my mom, and then she died, and I had no one. If something existed beside our mortal plane, I supposed it didn't care about me, or had a sick sense of fun. But when I saw you that first day and felt the mating bond tighten, I surmised any god would be the latter for sticking me with you."

"Wow, thanks." I laugh in annoyance.

He grabs my chin. "Then I actually listened to the words around your insults. I heard how much you cared for your people and how far you were willing to go to bring them justice. I envied you so damn much. I wish I had grown up surrounded by people like me, people who cared if I lived or died. I couldn't think clearly around you. One moment, I wanted far away from you. The next, I wanted inside of you. I think I knew the truth that night you cared for me when I was drunk. I was an idiot, trying to wash away my confusing feelings for you, knowing you were using me, and even though I didn't know the extent of it, I knew I cared for you and wanted you safe. But then you took care of me, even though you hated me and thought I was working with the Hunters. You could have demanded I reveal answers. I was so vulnerable, and yet you didn't take advantage of me. I realized it wasn't jealousy; it was a pounding want for more than just to knot you and further my genes, but to own a piece of your heart because you already held so much of mine without me even realizing you were taking it. I think now I'm optimistic about a higher power. Because damn, something magical had a hand in giving me such a perfect mate as you."

My eyes are blurry with tears, and I clench my mouth to hold back my sob. Damn him. Damn his words for doing this to me. His hands still dance over the skin on my face and my neck, and his eyes take me in. He's still attached to me, holding himself up as he looms over me. The emotions are too much, especially after the hormone dump from coming twice. I want to be vulnerable. I want to be soft, but instead, I part my lips and say, "I don't think I've ever heard you talk so much."

He narrows his eyes and shakes his head, pushing himself off of me as his knot deflates. I laugh at his annoyance, even if I regret my choice of words. I pull him back, cradling his jaw. "I never thought I'd have a mate either. I'm too stubborn. I believed in a higher power and thought if anyone was looking out for me than they wouldn't dare punish someone with a problem like me. I didn't feel the mating bond when I met you. I didn't expect it, so I assumed it was just a strong sexual charge between us. But I'd be lying if I said I didn't know before you told me. I think it was the day of the picnic—our first time. It snapped into place, but I pushed the realization away. It's been so short together, but I can see our future as clearly as I can see my past. Now I question if there's a god, because I don't deserve you. Why do some people suffer so much, and I can be immune from all that? I get to have you, and it's so not fair."

He smiles, his eyes almost clear of all their smoke. "You deserve everything." He smashes his mouth against mine. I'm unsure if it's because he can't resist being connected with me or if it's to make sure I don't ruin this beautiful moment by countering his statement. He's smart to do it either way. My hands crawl up his back, letting our words mix together as we seal them with a kiss.

He pulls back and raises an eyebrow. "It seems we have some conflicting religious views. Should we figure this out before having children?"

I pop a laugh. "Brick, if I know anything about us, I bet we have many more conflicting opinions than something as silly as religion. We have a lot to figure out before we have children."

He smirks down at me. "Can't wait."

My phone rings, and I groan with a stretch, reaching overhead until I feel it buried in the bed. It's probably time for both of us to get back to work. I answer without catching the caller, but once I hear their voice, I don't have to question. "It's time."

My heart stops.

23

HOUSE OF WOLVES

I'll never find them. After I turn a sharp corner and yet again discover another sterile white hall without any indication of where I'm going, I'm seconds away from giving up—from shifting and tearing down this place with fangs and claws. Brick grabs my arm, steadying my canine brain, reminding me there's no need for such dramatics. It's just a hospital.

I whirl to him, hoping he holds my answers. Sure enough, because he is annoyingly perfect, he points to the sign above the double set of doors. I breathe, turning toward the entryway, barreling down the new hall while reading the names next to each door.

Badson. I storm in, stopping once I enter, the sight before me leaving me breathless.

Red lay in the hospital bed, looking more beautiful than I have ever seen her. Her hair's a mess, and her face is puffy, but a glow shines through her pores. My brother hovers over her, looking so different, so at peace, so complete. He stares down at the bundle in Red's arms. When he pulls his eyes away to catch me, I feel immense guilt—how rude of me to interrupt this moment—but Cameron's smile doesn't falter. He stands, motioning for me to come closer. "Come meet your niece," he whispers.

I creep forward, feeling like a child again, unable to hold down the emotions tugging my heart every which way. Red doesn't look up until I'm standing next to her. "Isn't she perfect?"

I take her in. Truly perfection personified. The tiniest nose above a pair of lips. "She's so beautiful," I say, tears running down my cheeks. God this day is making me a softy.

"Do you want to hold her?" Red asks.

"Yes." I lean over to grab her from Red, immediately regretting my decision to take on such an immense responsibility. I'm going to drop her. "You're a natural," Red says, once the baby's safely in my arms. I roll my shoulders, letting the compliment ease my nerves. "What's her name?" I ask, not removing my gaze from her sweet face.

A silence passes and I glance up at Red and Cameron smiling at each other. "Christine Carmen Badson."

"No, shit?" My cheeks hurt from my smile, and tears completely fog my vision.

"Shit," Cameron replies.

I give a content sigh, still in disbelief at the angelic bundle in my arms. "Well, I hope for your two's sake she's less of an ass than her name suggests."

Red slaps my arm. "Hey! Her first name is my middle name."

I eye my brother. "Good luck, man."

Red laughs at that even as she mutters profanities under her breath.

I'd been so distracted that I completely forgot about my mate I left stranded in the hallway. "Come on in,"

Cameron says, and I turn to catch Brick hovering in the open doorway.

He enters, his head bowed. "Congratulations," he whispers, coming up from behind me and placing his hands on my shoulders.

"Isn't she beautiful?" I ask, staring up at him.

"So beautiful." He smiles down at her, a reverence and awe shining in his irises. Seeing him look at little Christine stirs something in me. Damn it.

As if listening to my ovaries, Cameron says, "You two are next."

My stomach drops. What a stupid-ass-brother thing to say to the man I've been seeing for mere weeks. And here I was, thinking fatherhood transformed him into something more respectable.

"Cameron!" Red scolded, just proving her best friend pedestal in my mind.

"One day," Brick says, rubbing his thumb over my protruding shoulder bone. Something shivers down my spine even as I try to catch it and push it away.

"We have to build our house of wolves. Keep the family strong," Cameron says, pumping his fist.

"What is this medieval times?" I snap.

"I might not fit in with the *House of Wolves,*" Brick says, angering me even more at my brother's words. Of course, Cameron knows that Brick isn't a werewolf but a werepig. He's been initiated in the pack regardless, even though Brick protested that he wouldn't fit in.

Cameron walks around the bed, slapping a hand on Brick's shoulders. "You're one of us. Welcome to the family."

It's touching to see my brother welcoming my mate into our family in the small hospital room filled with such joy, but also so cliche and kind of makes me want to puke. I do my best to stuff away a witty mark—something about how they should kiss on the lips to seal the family bond.

As if also being weirded out by the bro acceptance scene in front of us, Red clears her throat. Reaching for Christine, still in my arms. "Okay, enough of that. Back to telling me how cute my baby is and how awesome I am for pushing her out." That snaps Cameron out of it. He rushes to her side, kissing her cheek tenderly. "The most amazing thing I've ever seen and the cutest baby that has ever existed." He stares down at his daughter, shaking his head. "Sorry guys, it's going to be a tough competition."

"God, you're insufferable." I roll my eyes, even as Brick kisses down my neck and whispers in my ear. "We'll make the cutest piggy-wolves." I laugh, because he hates when I refer to him as a pig or a piggy. I twirl around, lacing my arms around his neck and kissing his lips. "Anything with you will be perfect."

"Couldn't agree more."

I smile against his lips. "Finally, something we agree on."

And just like that, it's a perfect day, filled with my favorite people, my favorite words, and the beginning of my new favorite love story.

And now that my new favorite person is Earthside, I have a kick-ass story to write to expose the shit out of the Hunters. Who cares what the Federal Dick-part-ment of Supernatural says? I've never been a rule fol-lower.

THANKS FOR READING

Thank you for reading! If you liked *House of Wolves: A Three Little Pigs Love Story* make sure to leave a review.

Want Grimm's story?

Bound to the Wolf: A Grimm Love Story

A cunning fox. A silver wolf. In a game of debts and deception, who will be the Hunter—and who will be the prey?

Twenty-year-old Ember is ready for a new start but unsure where to land. As she drives through the wooded town of Dayton, she's so distracted by the greenery around her that she completely misses the shiny red Porsche parked on the side of the road just around a bend. The now totaled car belongs to Grimm, a devastatingly attractive and terrifying man in his forties. He's furious and demands she repay him for the damages. Ember doesn't have a dollar to her name and now is without her only form of transportation or lodging.

Through his anger, Grimm finds an ounce of empathy, offering her to stay at a cottage on his property and work for him while she repays her debts. She agrees and finds herself thrust into a new and complicated living situation.

Grimm isn't just a charming silver fox. He's the Minister of a werewolf pack. He attempts to hide the truth about himself and his budding feelings for his new houseguest, but nothing can stay in the dark for long.

Ember has some secrets of her own. Maybe her mistakes weren't as accidental as they seemed, and maybe she's not as innocent as she looks.

The two find themselves forced to face their past prejudices, fears, and primal needs, thrusting them closer and closer together until the fire inside burns everything in its path.

Bound to the Wolf **can be enjoyed as a continuation of The Wolfish Love Stories or as a stand-alone.**

Stay up to date on all things G.M. Fairy!